The new kid walks in.

He's short. Real short. Kindergartner short. And he's wearing a gray suit with thin black stripes. And a black tie. Tell me that isn't weird—a kid wearing a suit and tie to school. Plus, he's wearing tiny, round wire-rimmed glasses over his very large eyes.

This is an extremely weird kid. Definitely weirder than me. Probably the weirdest in my school. Maybe the weirdest on earth.

Other Books by Patrick Jennings

ennings

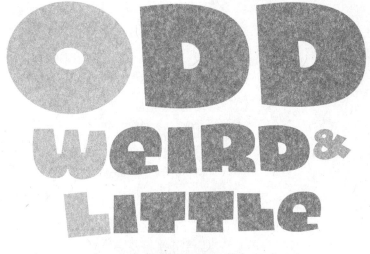

ODD
WEIRD&
LITTLE

EGMONT
—Publishing
NEW YORK

EGMONT

We bring stories to life

First published by Egmont USA, 2014
This paperback edition published by Egmont Publishing, 2015
443 Park Avenue South
New York, NY 10016
Copyright © 2014 by Patrick Jennings
All Rights Reserved

www.egmontusa.com
www.patrickjennings.com

1 3 5 7 9 8 6 4 2

This novel is based on the short story "Odd, Weird, and Little," by Patrick Jennings, which originally appeared in *Storyworks* magazine, January 2009.

THE LIBRARY OF CONGRESS HAS CATALOGED THE HARDCOVER EDITION AS FOLLOWS:
Jennings, Patrick.
Odd, weird & little / Patrick Jennings.
pages cm
Summary: Befriending a very strange new student, Toulouse, helps outsider Woodrow stand up to the class bullies who have been picking on them both.
ISBN 978-1-60684-374-1 (hardcover)
[1. Friendship—Fiction. 2. Eccentrics and eccentricities—Fiction.
3. Bullies—Fiction. 4. Middle schools—Fiction. 5. Schools—Fiction.]
I. Title.
PZ7.J4298715Odd 2014
[Fic]—dc23
2013018248
ISBN 978-1-60684-375-8 (eBook)
Paperback ISBN 978-1-60684-568-4

For Peter and Tate,
Original, Wise, and Loopy

Contents

ODD

WEIRD &

LITTLE

1. Our New Student

The new kid walks in.

"Excuse me, class," Mr. Logwood says. "Our new student has arrived. His name is Toulouse, and he just moved here from Quebec, which is a province of Canada. A province is like a state. His first language is French, but I'm told he's learning English quickly." He smiles down at the new boy.

None of us smile. We just stare at Toulouse.

He's short. Real short. Kindergartner short. And he's wearing a gray suit with thin black stripes. And a black tie. Tell me that isn't weird—a kid wearing a suit and tie to school. Plus, he's wearing tiny, round wire-rimmed glasses over his very large, round eyes. And an old-man hat. And black leather gloves.

And he's carrying a black briefcase. He kind of looks like my great-grandpa, only smaller. Way smaller.

This is an extremely weird kid. Definitely weirder than me. Probably the weirdest in our school. Maybe the weirdest on earth.

I glance over at Garrett Howell. He's grinning. Probably dreaming of terrible things to do to poor Toulouse.

I know what Garrett is capable of. I've been one of his victims for years now. Why? Maybe because I have orange hair and an overbite. I'm also clumsy, and sometimes I can't speak clearly, especially when I'm stressed. My words get all jammed up. I don't like dodgeball, tetherball, chasing games, or making fun of people. I do like to read books. I also keep lots of stuff in my pockets. I like to make things out of duck tape, and occasionally I wear things I make out of it: wristbands, bow ties, caps. . . . I insist on calling it *duck* tape, not *duct* tape, which is what most people call it. It was invented during World War II to waterproof ammunition. Waterproof. Duck. Duck tape.

I don't think any of this makes me weird. Compared to Toulouse, I'm practically normal.

"How . . . do . . . you . . . pronounce . . . your . . . last . . . name, Toulouse?" Mr. Logwood asks, as if pausing after every word will help the kid understand a foreign language. He writes Toulouse's full name on the whiteboard: "Toulouse Hulot."

Toulouse Hulot doesn't answer. He just stares.

"That's . . . okay," Mr. Logwood says. "You . . . can . . . tell . . . us . . . later. Would . . . you . . . like . . . to . . . hang . . . up . . . your . . . hat . . . and . . . coat?"

Toulouse shakes his head. Some of the kids giggle.

"That's . . . fine," Mr. Logwood says, though you're not allowed to wear a hat indoors at our school.

Mr. Logwood leads Toulouse over to our group. Toulouse stares at us, one at a time, his head swiveling, his eyes frozen in their sockets. It's creepy.

"Toulouse will be in your group, people.

Please introduce yourselves and help him feel at home." Mr. Logwood turns and walks away.

"Hi, I'm Monique," Monique Whitlow says.

"Ursula," says Ursula Lowry.

"Garrett," Garrett says, sticking out his hand like he wants to shake.

His henchman, Hubcap Ostwinkle, whose real name is Vitus Ostwinkle, snickers.

Garrett's up to something. Joy buzzer? Death grip? Did he slobber into his palm? I would not put anything past the guy.

When Toulouse holds out his gloved hand, Garrett jerks his own back and runs his fingers smoothly through his stubbly hair. The fake-out handshake. Never funny.

I take Toulouse's hand and shake it. His glove is soft and sewn together with heavy black stitches. There's something strange about the way his hand feels inside it, as if it's too small, too light. His bones feel thin and fragile. I grip his hand gently, just in case.

"I'm . . . ," I say, then momentarily forget my name. "Woodrow Schwette?" I say it like a question.

Hubcap snorts like a donkey. *Donkey* is a polite word for what he is.

Toulouse makes a little bow in my direction. Which is odd, but also sort of classy.

He hops up onto his chair. His feet don't reach the floor.

"Name's Hubcap," Hubcap says. "You're really short, kid."

So rude.

"Please take out your writing notebooks, class," Mr. Logwood announces. "Today we are going to write about how it might feel to be a new student in a new classroom. Of course, Toulouse, you ... can ... write ... about ... how ... it ... *does* ... feel ... to ... be ... a ... new ... student."

Toulouse sets his briefcase on his desk, unsnaps its two silver buckles, and takes out a small, square black bottle, a white feather, and a book with a plain black cover. He unscrews the top of the bottle and dips the pointy end of the feather into it.

Monique and Ursula stare at him like he just climbed out of a flying saucer. Ursula actually points.

Toulouse opens the black book and begins writing. It must be a journal of some kind. The feather—a quill?—makes scratchy noises as he drags it across the paper. He stops every few words or so to redip.

Nobody else writes. We all watch him. He doesn't seem to notice. Or care.

No doubt about it: he's weird. But in a weirdly cool way.

2. Weirder Than Woody

At recess everyone is talking about Toulouse.

Everyone but me. I'm not talking to anyone, nor is anyone talking to me. They're all talking together by the swing set, and I'm hanging by my knees from the climbing structure next to them, the one that's a ladder that goes up, then bends horizontally, then bends back down, ending up on the ground again. Climb it and you end up no higher than you started. A pointless ladder. A ladder to nowhere.

I do listen, though.

Monique says, "He never speaks."

Ursula: "He doesn't speak *English*."

Monique: "He has a *briefcase*."

Ursula: "He keeps an *ink bottle* in his briefcase."

Garrett: "He wears a *suit*."

Hubcap: "Yeah! And a *tie*."

Ursula: "His eyes are *huge*."

Monique: "He's little."

Ursula: "He's odd."

Garrett: "He's seriously *weird*. Look at him!"

Hubcap: "Yeah, look at him!"

He points at a tree at the edge of the playground. Toulouse is perched on a high branch, reading.

I jump down from the Ladder to Nowhere and walk over to Toulouse's tree. He's holding an old hardcover book, the kind without a jacket. It looks enormous in his tiny lap.

"Excuse me? Toulouse?" I call to him. "I'm Woodrow? You know . . . from . . . I'm in your group?"

He looks up from his book and says, "Who?" It's the first word I've heard him say. His voice is whispery and hollow. Kind of ghostlike. Kind of flutey. Kind of spooky.

"Woodrow?" I say again. "I'm in . . . I sit next . . . you don't remember?"

He nods yes, then sits waiting for me to say

something else. The problem is that I don't have anything else. Striking up conversations is not something I'm good at.

So we stare at each other for a while.

Quite a while.

Then at last I think of something to say.

"I like your hat."

He nods thank you.

"What's that you're reading?" I ask. I'm warming up.

He turns the book toward me, though I'm not sure why. I can't possibly read its title from way down here.

"Is it good?"

He nods yes.

I run out of things to say again, so we go back to staring.

In time, the bell rings. Toulouse doesn't move.

"That means it's time to . . . you know . . . go in?"

I look away, point to the students all rushing to get in line. When I look back, he's not on his branch anymore. I gasp. I mean, the guy was really high. Did he fall?

No. He's standing next to me. How did he get down so fast?

We walk together toward the others. Toulouse comes up to my elbow, even with his hat on.

"Hey, Woody!" Garrett howls. "I think you finally found someone weirder than you!"

He always calls me Woody. He's the only one who does, except Hubcap, who repeats everything Garrett says.

"Yeah, Woody!" Hubcap echoes. "Even weirder than you!"

Toulouse seems calm, like being insulted doesn't bother him. I've lived in this country since I was born, and have gone to Uwila Elementary since kindergarten, and I still get upset when Garrett taunts me. I'm impressed how Toulouse doesn't let him ruffle his feathers.

"Ignore them," I whisper.

"Who?" he says.

"Exactly," I say.

3. Learning to Watercolor

After recess is art. Ms. Wolf sets a big basket filled with fruit and flowers on a stool in the center of the room—a still life, she calls it—and we sit in a circle and paint it.

She's been trying to show us how to use watercolors properly. She says we shouldn't swirl our brushes in the plastic jar of water then go straight to the tiny hockey pucks of paint. That just makes a mess and blends all the colors into a dull, dark purplish-brown. What we're supposed to do is dip the tip of our brush into the water, dab away most of the water on a piece of paper towel, go to the pucks for paint, then mix it on the plastic plate with the little compartments. Once we have the color we want, we brush it on the paper.

For most of us, though, the fun isn't in painting the fruit and flowers. It's in swirling our brushes in the jar of water and watching the colors change, then slopping the water onto the pucks and watching the paint run and mix. The fun is in making a sloppy, colorful mess.

Most of our paintings are dark purplish-brown puddles. Our sheets of paper are soaked and pucker and start to peel. But we don't mind. We're expressing ourselves, which Ms. Wolf is always telling us we should do. We express ourselves in messes.

Ms. Wolf hurries around the classroom in her apron, complaining. "No, no, that's too much! . . . Easy does it! . . . One color at a time! . . . Get more paper towels! Quickly!"

In the middle of this chaos, I notice Toulouse, sitting off by himself, next to the window. There isn't enough room for an extra kid at the tables. We have a big class.

Toulouse's paper is sitting upright on a little wooden tripod, an easel, that he got out of his briefcase. Who carries an easel in a briefcase? Who carries an easel, period? Or a briefcase?

Toulouse carefully dips his brush into the jar of water, dabs it on a folded paper towel, touches the tip to one of the color pucks, mixes it in one of the plastic plate compartments, then paints. I can't see his picture from where I'm sitting, and we're not supposed to get out of our seats. I'd really like to see it, but rules are rules.

When it's nearly time to go, Ms. Wolf says, "Okay, class, please begin cleaning up. *Carefully*."

All of us stop painting at once and dunk our brushes deep into the jars to clean them. We swish them violently. Hubcap knocks over the one on our table. Ursula squeals. Monique snatches her painting and holds it over her head so it won't get wet. I doubt a little water could make it look any worse.

We are now allowed to leave our seats, but only to carry our paintings over to the windowsill and lay them out to dry. After I do, I walk over to Toulouse. He's carefully drying his brushes with sheets of paper towel.

"I love your easel," I say, then glance at his painting. It is so good! You can actually see the pears and apples and the pink flowers and the basket they're sitting in. They look almost real. Not like a photograph, though. They look realer.

"Toulouse!" I say, then can't think of anything else to say.

"Look at Toulouse's painting!" Monique says.

The noise level in the room drops, and people start wandering over.

"Keep cleaning up now!" Ms. Wolf says, clapping her hands. "We're not finished! Clean up, please!"

"Ms. Wolf!" Monique says. "You have to come see Toulouse's painting!"

"Later, Monique," Ms. Wolf says. She picks up two Mason jars of water, one in each hand. "Everyone now! Please keep cleaning up!"

"But Ms. Wolf," Ursula says, after she's looked at Toulouse's painting, "you really should look. It's *amazing*."

"Ursula, you really should be *cleaning*," Ms. Wolf replies. "I'll look at it after we've finished."

No one is listening to her. Everyone has

slowly gathered around Toulouse's picture. When Ms. Wolf sees this, she stomps over, sloshing the water in the jars she's holding.

"Really, children, you need to be—"

She sees Toulouse's painting. Her mouth falls open, and the jars of dark purplish-brown water crash to the floor.

4. Outside

"Did you see his painting?" Monique asks Ursula on the playground after lunch. Ursula and Monique are swinging on swings.

Ursula: "Yes. It was a masterpiece. Like a Rembrandt."

Monique: "More like a Matisse."

Hubcap: "What's that?"

Ursula: "Don't you remember? Ms. Wolf showed us paintings of his. The ones with the fruit?"

Garrett: "I don't get painting fruit. By the time you finish it, it's rotten and you can't eat it."

Hubcap: "Right! This Matisse guy must have wasted a lot of food!"

Monique: "The fruit was plastic."

Ursula: "So were the flowers."

Monique: "Toulouse's painting was as good as Matisse's."

Ursula: "I don't know. Matisse was a great artist. Toulouse is just a kid."

Garrett: "Just a *weird* kid."

Hubcap: "Exactly. Weird."

Monique: "You're just jealous."

Garrett: "Jealous? Of being able to paint fruit?"

Hubcap: "Who wants to paint fruit?"

Garrett: "Not me."

Hubcap: "Me, neither."

Ursula: "Did you see Toulouse hop up on the supply cabinet?"

Garrett: "Yeah, the scaredy-cat."

Hubcap: "Scaredy-cat! Afraid of a little water!"

Monique: "He wasn't afraid. He was protecting his painting."

Garrett: "He was chicken."

Monique: "Which is he: a chicken or a cat?"

Hubcap: "Both! Right, Garrett?"

Garrett: "Yeah, both. Plus, he's weird."

Ursula: "Maybe he's a genius."

Garrett: "A genius? How can he be a genius when he can't even talk?"

Hubcap: "Yeah! He can't even talk!"

Ursula: "He can talk. He just can't speak *English*."

Garrett: "And what kind of name is Toulouse? 'To *lose*,' more like."

Hubcap: "Yeah! 'To be a loser'! Right, Garrett?"

Garrett: "Right. Let's play some tetherball, Hub."

Hubcap: "Lead the way."

They walk away, laughing and punching and elbowing each other.

Monique and Ursula keep swinging. Monique glances up at me as she reaches my height. I'm sitting on the Ladder to Nowhere, eavesdropping.

"Maybe they, like . . . ," I say. "Maybe in Quebec . . . they teach watercolor . . . teach kids how to . . . you know . . . paint . . . really young . . . maybe in kindergarten," I say.

Monique shrugs, glances away, then, having hit the peak of her swing, drops backward and away.

5. Walking Up a Tree

I climb down from the Ladder and walk over to Toulouse's tree.

I have to tilt my head to see him. He's sitting on the same branch with his briefcase open in his lap. He peeks around it and looks down at me. Ursula's right about one thing: he has huge eyes. Even from this distance they're weirdly big.

"Hi," I say.

"Who?" he says.

Maybe *who* is *hi* in French?

"It's me, Woodrow. Can I come up?"

He stares a few seconds, long enough to make me feel uneasy, then blinks a couple of times. Is that a yes?

I reach up for the lowest branch, but it's

too high. I hop for it. Nope. How did Toulouse reach it?

I pull some cord out of my pocket. It's good to keep some nylon cord with you. You never know when it will come in handy. I have a coil of about four feet in length. I found this piece in our backyard. It's probably part of some-body's old clothesline. It's pale yellow and fraying, but it's still strong.

I tie one end around a flat stone, then fling it up at the branch. It passes over and swings back down and conks me in the forehead. I see stars for a while, but then I'm all right.

I untie the stone and wrap the ends of the cord around my hands a few times, then tug them till they're taut, and begin walking up the tree trunk, Batman-style. The bark is slipperier than I thought it'd be, though. I try walking faster, but I get no higher. I'm speed skating horizontally on a tree trunk. Meanwhile, the cord tightens and starts cutting into my hands. Above me, where it's rubbing against the branch, it starts to split. Finally, it snaps, and I fall to the ground. I land on my back with a thud.

I don't see stars. I see leaves, branches, and bits of sky. I think you see stars only when you get hit on the head. The fall knocked the air out of me, though. I just stay flat on my back, close my eyes, and wait for my breath to return.

"Woodrow?"

He knows my name.

I open my eyes, and he's standing right next to me. How does he do that?

"I'm all right," I tell him. "Well, not *all* right . . . but I'm . . . I'm not badly injured or anything."

His head tilts slightly, like he's confused.

"I fall all the time," I say. "My body's . . . used to it."

I'm lucky I fell on my back, since most of the stuff I'm carrying is stuffed into my front pockets. The metal pencil sharpener, for example, and a couple of small rolls of duck tape, an empty mint tin, and a Ticonderoga, which is my favorite pencil. I do have one roll of red duck tape in my back pocket, however, which didn't feel good to land on.

Toulouse reaches out a gloved hand. He's

holding his briefcase in his other one.

I gently take his hand and pretend to let him pull me to a sitting position. I doubt he could do it. He's pretty short.

"Thanks. Sorry I . . . you know . . . interrupted your lunch." I point at his case.

He just stares, like he doesn't understand what I'm saying.

"Your . . . lunch?" I say. Now I sound like Mr. Logwood. I pretend I'm eating by moving my hand to my mouth and making biting and chewing motions. "Lunch? Meal? Food? I'm sorry?"

He lets go of my hand and takes a watch from his pocket that is attached to his vest by a chain. He squeezes it, and the brass cover pops open, which is cool. He reads the time and nods, then snaps the watch shut and slips it back in his pocket. He looks at the building.

The bell rings.

I get to my feet and try to reach around to brush the dirt off my back. Toulouse removes a little whisk broom from inside his jacket and helps me out. The guy has cool stuff.

"Thanks," I say.

He stops brushing and puts the whisk broom back in his coat.

"Your still life was . . ." I can't think of the right word to describe what I think his painting was. It was amazing, beautiful, and surprising. Is there one word for all that?

He stares at me. I swear his eyes are as big and round as the roll of tape in my back pocket.

"It was . . . you know . . . it was super-something . . . not super-duper . . . super . . . um . . . uh . . . su*perb*?"

He gives me a little bow. He understands.

I bow back.

6. Logwood Sings

"Ms. . . . Wolf . . . tells . . . me . . . you . . . are . . . quite . . . the . . . artist," Mr. Logwood says to Toulouse when we're back in the classroom.

Toulouse doesn't answer.

"He's an *amazing* artist," Monique says. "You should see his painting."

"Of fruit," Garrett says under his breath.

Hubcap snickers.

"Respect, gentlemen," Mr. Logwood says. "Do you need me to sing it for you?"

"No!" Garrett and Hubcap say in unison.

The song Mr. Logwood sings is an old one my parents listen to sometimes. Mr. Logwood doesn't sing very well, though.

"Then please get out your math materials while I collect some for Toulouse."

"Who?" Toulouse says at the mention of his name.

Garrett and Hubcap snicker.

Mr. Logwood begins singing the old song.

"Okay! Sorry! *Sorry!*" Garrett says.

Hubcap: "Yeah, we're *so* sorry!"

Mr. Logwood ends the song. "Math materials, gentlemen," he says, then gets some for Toulouse.

We've been studying shapes. Triangles. Polygons. Quadrilaterals. When Toulouse gets today's handout, which is called, "Greater Than Right: Obtuse Angles," he opens his briefcase and takes out: a steel ruler with etched markings and a cork backing; a steel protractor (also etched); a pink rubber eraser; and three yellow, unsharpened pencils (Ticonderogas!). I dig the sharpener out of my pocket. It's a heavy, bronze cylinder (speaking of geometric shapes . . .) about an inch in diameter with a sharp metal blade on the top. I love it, and I'm hoping Toulouse will appreciate its fine workmanship.

"Would you like this . . . to use?" I ask him. "The one on the wall . . . it's terrible. It mangles your Ticonderogas."

He stares at me.

Too much English?

I hold the sharpener out and smile.

He sticks out his gloved hand, palm up. I set the sharpener in it. He bounces his hand, weighing it, then he picks it up with the gloved fingers of his other hand and inspects it. One of his eyes close, and I notice a strange thing: just before his eyelids touch, a dark diagonal line appears between them, over his large iris. Does he wear contacts?

When he's finished looking the sharpener over—I can tell he appreciates the workmanship—he slides one of his pencils into the smaller of the two sharpening ports and twists it. The painted skin of the Ticonderoga curls over the blade like an apple peel.

I dig into my other pocket and take out the small, empty mint tin, then pop it open with my thumb. It still smells of peppermint.

"For the shavings," I say.

He nods and shakes the shavings loose. They flutter down into the tin.

"This is so sweet," Garrett says.

"Touching," Hubcap adds.

"Two dorks in love."

"Dork love."

Garrett makes a little kissing sound. Hubcap joins in.

I suddenly wonder whether being friendly to Toulouse is such a good idea. Garrett claims Toulouse is weirder than me. If I become friends with him, what will that say about me? If I distance myself from Toulouse, maybe Garrett will finally leave me alone.

Toulouse lowers his hands and stares at Garrett's puckering mouth, then pivots his head and stares at Hubcap's.

"Stop staring at me, freak," Hubcap says, squirming.

Toulouse makes a sound with his mouth. I think he's trying to make a kissing sound, but it ends up sounding more clicky than kissy.

"I think he wants a kiss, Hub," Garrett says.

Hubcap: "Well, he's not getting one."

"Leave him alone, Garrett," Monique says.

I was going to say that, but it got stuck in my throat.

Toulouse hands the sharpener back to me with a thank-you nod, then takes a small notepad with a brown leather cover out of his briefcase and flips it open. He scribbles something on the pad, tears off the sheet, and passes it to Garrett.

We all lean in to read it. In fancy cursive, it reads:

Avoid obtuseness.

7. Obtuse

So he knows some English. Some pretty fancy English, actually.

Maybe he's only learned to read and write it, though. Maybe he can't speak it.

Obtuse is on our math handout: "Greater Than Right: Obtuse Angles." It's an angle greater than ninety degrees but less than one hundred eighty. That is, it's between a right angle and a straight line.

I'm pretty sure that's not what Toulouse meant by *obtuseness*, though. Maybe he's being clever. Maybe the word has other meanings.

During Silent Sustained Reading, I look it up in the dictionary. It lists two meanings for *obtuse*. One is about angles. The other definition is "blunt or dull." Toulouse was telling Garrett to avoid dullness, to be sharp, which Garrett definitely wasn't being.

Toulouse is the sharp one.

I go back to my seat. Everybody's reading. Monique's book is called *The Witch Family*. Ursula's is *Calling on Dragons*. Garrett's is a nonfiction picture book about weapons called *Arms and Armor*. Hubcap is flipping through another in the same series. It's called *Combat*. Toulouse is reading the same book he had in the tree, which is called *Nonsense Songs, Stories, Botany, and Alphabets*. Botany?

He has the book lying on his desk, so I can see there are drawings in it. Cartoons. Black-and-white line drawings. They look goofy, like the ones in my book. (I'm reading Captain Underpants, the one about the teacher who gives wedgies.) The words in Toulouse's book are in English, which doesn't surprise me, since the title is in English, too.

Toulouse also has a small, paperback French/English dictionary on his desk, which he took out of his briefcase. That case sure holds a lot of stuff.

I try to focus on my book, but I can't seem to stop spying on Toulouse. He reads with his eyes opened so wide it's like he's watching a scary movie. And his eyes don't move left to right when he reads. They stare straight ahead. His head moves instead. When he finishes a line, his head snaps back to the beginning.

He laughs a couple of times—just little hoots—then he quickly covers his mouth with his hand and glances around to see if anyone noticed. Both times, I dive behind my book. I don't fool him the second time. He waits for me to come out, then he spins his book around and slides it toward me.

On the page is a drawing of some round-faced kids aboard a circular boat with a white flag flying from a mast in the center. It's sailing in a choppy sea, and some of the kids have their hands up in the air, like they're excited. The others look angry, or worried.

Under the drawing is a poem. It's called "The Jumblies." These Jumbly people went to sea in a sieve. I'm pretty sure a sieve is like a colander, something you use to drain liquid, like from pasta or beans. A bowl filled with holes, in other words. No wonder some of them look worried, or angry.

The poem rhymes, which seems babyish to me, and has a chorus at the end of each verse about how the Jumblies have green heads and blue hands, which is sort of funny but also kind of babyish. I figure if I was learning a new language, I might have to read books like this. But Toulouse understands words like *obtuseness*. This book must be too basic for him, so he must read it because he likes it.

I look at him and smile politely. Then I open my book to a particularly funny page and slide it to him. I feel a little bad that mine is so much funnier, but this is America, and he might as well get used to how good things can be here.

He stares down at the book.

And stares.

And stares.

Amazingly, he doesn't laugh. Maybe he doesn't get the humor. Maybe what's funny in Quebec and what's funny here are different.

He turns the page and keeps staring. A

minute later, he flips to the next page. Then the next one. Then he looks up at me. And hoots. I jump. Everyone jumps. It wasn't that loud a hoot. It's just that SSR time is pretty quiet.

He looks a little worried, like one of the Jumblies in the boat.

I probably should have warned him how funny the book is.

8. Wire, Feathers, and Hooks

Toulouse obviously loves Otto and Billy Bob, our goldfish.

They live on the windowsill next to Mr. Logwood's desk in a classic fishbowl: round, but flat on the sides, not spherical. (This geometry stuff is really sinking in.) They must be so bored. They putter around the bowl, fluttering their fins, passing each other without seeming to notice, or care. Now and then Otto will chase Billy Bob around, nipping at his tail fin.

I wonder if they like each other. Or hate each other. I think about being stuck in a glass bowl with Garrett. That would be more awful than the most awful thing in the universe. Well, unless Hubcap was in there, too.

If I had to be cooped up in a fishbowl forever with someone, I'd prefer it be Toulouse.

It's funny I feel this way, considering I just met him this morning. I guess so far I like him. It seems as if he likes me. It'd be great to have a friend, but I don't know if he would be such a great choice. Weird plus weird might make us double weird. Or triple. I'd get picked on, he'd get picked on, we'd get picked on—and by both Garrett and Hubcap. So that would be double triple. Six times the taunting. I should probably back off befriending Toulouse.

I mean, look at him. He's been staring at the fish so long that he's starting to attract attention. Lots of kids are watching him watch. I guess he really likes fish. Some people do.

For example, me. I'm not interested in goldfish in a bowl. It's depressing. But I like to catch them. I like fishing. What I really like doing is making lures and flies. I like assembling the wire and feathers and hooks.

We're supposed to be writing a chapter summary of the book we read during SSR, but I whisper, "Do you like to fish?"

He jumps and makes a peep sound.

"Sorry," I say. "I just saw . . . noticed . . . you're staring . . ."

Toulouse nods but continues to stare at the fishbowl.

"So do you like to fish?" I ask.

He nods again.

"Do you make your own lures?"

Another nod.

"Do you own a rod . . . tackle?"

He turns his head slowly and stares at me. Do his eyes *ever* move in their sockets? Maybe something is wrong with them. I probably shouldn't ask till I get to know him better.

"Oui," he says.

He definitely understands a lot more English than Mr. Logwood gives him credit for. I don't understand any French, but I know *oui* means yes.

He opens his briefcase and reaches inside. He's taken so much stuff out of it, I half expect him to pull out a floor lamp, like Mary Poppins did in the movie, but all he takes out is a small, gray, metal, hinged case. A case in a case. He opens the metal clasp. Inside are feathers, fur, hooks, fishing line, wire, and various tools. The case is a tackle box! He lifts out a perfect dragonfly with a glittering blue-sequined body.

I reach my hand up and close my mouth. I guess it fell open. I can't believe what I'm seeing. I've met a couple of kids who make lures and flies. I've never met one who carries tackle around with him.

Is there no way he and I can become friends? Curse you, Garrett Howell! You, too, Hubcap Ostwinkle!

Toulouse hands me the dragonfly, and, after looking around for Mr. Logwood (he's talking with a kid on the other side of the room), I take it. It's really fine work. Strong and beautiful. I wish I could try it out on real fish. I wish I was at the creek right now with Toulouse and our rods.

"We should go . . . do . . . do you want . . . I think we . . . ," I stammer. "There's a creek . . . we could . . . you know . . . fish at?"

He stares at me. No surprise there. But

he stares long enough this time that I begin to wonder if he's trying to think of some way to get out of going fishing with me without hurting my feelings. Then I wonder if he understood me. I mean, sure, he understands English okay, but was what I said really English?

I try again.

"Want to go fishing sometime?"

He stares.

I take this as a no. "Or not . . . no, you're probably . . . maybe you don't . . ."

"Okay," he says, a bit too loudly.

"Hey, he spoke," Monique says.

"Whoa," Garrett says. "He knows a whole word in English."

"Yeah, one whole word," Hubcap says.

I want to point out that Toulouse has also said "who" and my name, but I don't.

"Is that all you can say, little guy?" Garrett asks Toulouse. "Just one word?"

Toulouse stares at him. He blinks. Slowly. I see those funny diagonal lines flash in his eyes again.

"Yes," he says in his flutey little voice. "I can speak only the one."

Whether we become friends or not, I really like this guy.

9. Ladder to Nowhere

Toulouse and I sit on top of the Ladder to Nowhere during afternoon recess, making lures. He has terrific tools in his little tackle box: tweezers, needles, needle-nose pliers, superglue, and wire cutters. He shows me how to make the dragonfly, and I promise to show him how to make a grasshopper with an orange abdomen, which is one of my specialties.

Garrett and Hubcap walk up. Here comes the taunting times six.

"You guys making pretty jewelry?" Garrett asks, looking up at us.

Hubcap: "Pretty bracelets, maybe, to give each other on Valentine's Day?"

"It's October," I say.

"But you guys are in love, right?" Garrett

says, then starts singing, "'Woody and Weirdy . . . sitting in a tree . . .'"

Hubcap laughs, then chimes in.

Toulouse looks at me, confused.

If kids don't sing this song in Quebec, I want to move to Quebec.

"'. . . then comes Woody in a baby carriage,'" they finish, then bust up laughing.

"Isn't it supposed to be 'with a baby carriage'?" Ursula asks. She's swinging next to the Ladder. "I mean, is Woodrow the baby or the mom?"

"Does it matter?" Garrett asks.

Hubcap: "Maybe both!"

He reaches up and grabs a loose thread hanging from Toulouse's kit, twirls it around his finger a few times, then tugs it. The spool it's attached to bounces out of the kit. Toulouse strains to catch it, loses his balance, and starts falling forward. I reach out for him and end up slipping off the rung I'm sitting on. I catch myself with my knees, but my back slams against the rung behind me. I hook the bar with my arms. I'm stuck like a crab going down a drain, my arms and legs flailing.

Toulouse's kit and briefcase fall and land in the sand. Garrett and Hubcap pounce on them.

I look around for Toulouse, but he's no longer on the Ladder. He's also not below me on the ground. I scan the playground. There he is, perched atop the swing set, over Ursula's head. How'd he get up there? And so fast?

He sits there, watching Garrett and Hubcap as they go through his things. He's too polite, I think, to complain. Or maybe too scared.

I feel angry. Really angry. It's bad enough when Garrett and Hubcap are mean to me, but it stinks when they pick on poor little Toulouse. I can't not do something.

I unhook my arms and drop through the rungs till I'm hanging upside down from my knees, right above Garrett. I swing my arm down and snatch the handle of the briefcase, which causes it to slam shut. Garrett pulls his fingers out just in time. Too bad. I pull myself back up to safety. It was a daring and successful rescue operation, carried out fairly flawlessly.

I don't know where I found the bravery and flair, but I'm happy I did.

"Give that back!" Garrett says, jumping to his feet.

Hubcap leaps up and orders me to give it back, too. He's holding Toulouse's tackle box in his hand.

"Put that . . . ," I say. "That doesn't belong . . . Put it down!"

"It doesn't belong to you, either," Garrett says.

Hubcap: "Yeah!"

"Hey, where'd Weirdy go?" Garrett asks, looking around.

Hubcap: "Yeah. Where'd Loser go?"

I try not to look at the swing set.

The bell rings. I'm saved by it.

Hubcap drops the tackle box, then gives it a kick. The two of them then run off toward the building.

I drop to the ground. The tackle box is still closed. It's not dented or anything. I dust it off on my pant leg.

"*Merci*," Toulouse says.

I scream. How did he get here so fast?

"What did you say?" I ask.

"*Merci,*" he repeats. "Thank you."

"Oh. How do you say 'you're welcome' in French?"

"*De rien.*"

I repeat it the best I can.

"Good!" he says.

"*Merci,*" I say.

10. Ottoless

"So . . . Toulouse," Mr. Logwood says when we're back inside, "I've . . . noticed . . . you . . . like . . . the . . . goldfish. Would . . . you . . . like . . . to . . . feed . . . them?"

Toulouse nods enthusiastically, then hustles over on his short legs to the window beside Mr. Logwood's desk. The bowl is at his eye level. He presses his pointy little nose against the glass. I hear a clink. Must be his glasses.

Mr. Logwood hands him the fish food.

"We . . . give . . . them . . . two . . . shakes," he says.

I wonder if I should tell him he doesn't need to speak slowly to Toulouse, that Toulouse understands.

Nah, he's a teacher, he'll figure it out.

After giving Toulouse the fish food shaker, Mr. Logwood gets a step stool from the supply closet, but by the time he returns with it, Toulouse has hopped up onto the windowsill. We're not allowed on the windowsills.

Mr. Logwood laughs uncomfortably. "Okay. I . . . don't . . . usually . . . allow . . . students . . . up . . . there. Promise . . . you . . . will . . . be . . . careful?"

Toulouse doesn't answer. He leans his face over the fishbowl. His nose is practically touching the water. His eyes are opened very wide. He shakes some fish flakes into the bowl. They float on the surface. Usually Otto and Billy Bob rush up to eat them, but not this time. They swim in panicky circles at the bottom of the bowl.

The whole class is watching, spellbound.

"Okay," Mr. Logwood says. "Thank . . . you, Toulouse."

He holds out his hand. Is it for the shaker or to help Toulouse down? Toulouse does not need help getting down, that's for sure, but Mr. Logwood doesn't know that.

Toulouse hands him the fish food shaker, still not taking his eyes off the fish. He does not jump down from the windowsill.

Mr. Logwood coughs, then turns to us. "I believe we have a spelling test planned for now."

Garrett groans.

"Do I need to sing the respect song for you, Mr. Howell?" Mr. Logwood asks.

"No, no," Garrett says, painting a smile on his face. "I'd love to take a spelling test, Mr. Logwood."

He really doesn't like it when Mr. Logwood sings.

None of us are paying much attention to this conversation. For one thing, we've all heard it a million times. For another, Toulouse is still leaning over the fishbowl, gazing down at the frightened Otto and Billy Bob.

Sensing that everyone is staring at Toulouse, Mr. Logwood leans over and whispers in his ear, "Please . . . take . . . your . . . seat . . . now."

Toulouse doesn't move. He doesn't want to take his seat. He doesn't want to leave the fish. He likes the fish. Maybe he wants to catch them. He likes fishing. He makes his own lures. He carries a tackle box around with him.

But he wouldn't want to catch Otto and Billy Bob, would he? He wouldn't *eat* them? I mean, they're *gold*fish. They're pets.

I stand up and walk over to him.

"Come on," I say. "Come sit down."

Garrett snickers, then Hubcap does. Toulouse and I may as well go ahead and be friends now. That's how Garrett and Hubcap see us. And they're loving it.

"That's enough of that, boys," Mr. Logwood says in his deep, no-nonsense voice. "It's not easy adjusting to a new culture. We need to be compassionate and welcoming." He turns to me. "As Woodrow is being. Thank you, Woodrow."

I gesture "you're welcome" by lifting one shoulder then dropping it. I hook Toulouse's arm and give it a tug. He's as light as a feather. I lead him back to our desks.

"'K-I-S-S-I-N-G . . . ,'" Hubcap whisper-sings out of the corner of his mouth.

"Vitus," Mr. Logwood says. "I'm going to

need you to take a Think Time at the back of the room, please."

Hubcap jumps up and moves through the desks, pretending he doesn't care—grinning, fake-gagging, eye-rolling—but it's obvious he's embarrassed.

I don't get Hubcap, or Garrett. It's like they go out of their way to be mean, like they're proud of getting in trouble.

Toulouse and I sit down. I doubt Toulouse will have to take the spelling test. He didn't get the word list Mr. Logwood handed out yesterday. I didn't study it much, but I do remember it had tricky words with *i-e* or *e-i*: *believe, deceive, neighbor, seize. . . .*

"*Oh!*" Ursula screams. She points at the fishbowl. "Where's Otto?"

11. Weirdness Factor

Everyone stares at Toulouse. He stares back, at one person at a time, in that odd, wide-eyed, head-pivoting way of his. He looks at the kids sitting behind him by twisting his head all the way around without turning his body. This adds to his weirdness factor. I don't think anyone is breathing.

We had all watched him gape at the fish. We'd all seen how he refused to walk away from them. No one claims they saw him touch Otto. We had all been distracted by Hubcap getting a Think Time. I had been standing right next to Toulouse. I didn't see him get up from his chair. But I was distracted by Hubcap, too. Not for long, but, knowing how fast Toulouse can move, it could have been long enough for him to . . . to . . .

But he couldn't have. He just *couldn't*. He isn't wet in the slightest. Wouldn't his gloves be wet? They aren't.

Besides, why would he steal a fish from a fishbowl?

"Did . . . you . . . see . . . what . . . happened . . . to . . . Otto?" Mr. Logwood asks Toulouse in a soft, patient voice.

Toulouse stares at him.

"Otto!" Ursula says. "You know, our *fish*!"

"He doesn't speak English," someone says.

"Yes, he does," Garrett says. "I heard him say a lot of English words."

Everybody starts whispering.

"Quiet, please," Mr. Logwood says, raising a hand. "Toulouse, is this true?" he says without any pauses. "Can you understand me?"

All the attention has caused Toulouse to sink down in his chair, which makes him look even smaller. He gives a tiny nod.

"See?" Garrett snarls. "He understands English good enough."

"*Well* enough," Monique says.

Mr. Logwood coughs. He always does this

when he's preparing to redirect our attention. "Time for the spelling test. Clear your desks. Get out a sheet of writing paper and something to write with, please."

Everyone groans. Everyone, that is, except Toulouse. He sighs. Is he relieved?

"But what about Otto?" Ursula asks.

"We'll deal with that later," Mr. Logwood says without looking at her. "It's time for spelling."

He leans over Toulouse, and says quietly, "Obviously, you can't take the test. Please wait for me over there, in the Gathering Place, and I'll bring you the list. You can follow along as I read the words aloud."

Toulouse hops down from his chair and heads toward the Gathering Place, an area with a circular rug for us students and a short, stuffed armchair for Mr. Logwood. It's where we sit and share.

Toulouse hops into the chair. There's a loud gasp.

"Actually, Toulouse," Mr. Logwood says with a strained smile, "that chair is reserved for me."

Toulouse climbs down and sits on the rug.

Mr. Logwood hands him a list of the spelling words. Toulouse stands up and looks around, as if he lost something. Then he starts walking back toward his desk. I see why: he forgot his briefcase. It's on the floor by his chair.

"Where are you going, Toulouse?" Mr. Logwood asks.

"He forgot his briefcase," I say.

"I see," Mr. Logwood says, then to us, asks, "Are we ready? Let's begin the test. The first word is *weird*."

We all start writing. *Weird* sure is a weird word. It breaks the *i* before *e* rule. It should be spelled *wierd*.

When I finish writing it and look up, Toulouse is back in the Gathering Place with his briefcase. I didn't notice him pick it up, or even come near his desk. The kid moves so silently.

"Hey!" Ursula says, pointing. "He's back! Otto's back in the bowl!"

12. Latin

After spelling, we go to choir. We walk single file down the hall, Mr. Logwood in the lead, then Toulouse, then me and the rest of our class, which means everyone is whispering about Toulouse behind his back. I've done enough dumb stuff in the past to know how that feels, like the time I pretended to be a badger and put chopsticks in my mouth and ended up with them jammed down my throat. Everyone whispered behind my back for a couple of days after that one.

Not that Toulouse did a dumb thing. I don't know what he did, and neither does anyone else. I admit it's suspicious, but there's no proof he had anything to do with Otto's disappearance. Or reappearance.

Unfortunately, getting judged for things you didn't do is part of life for a kid who gets picked on.

I feel bad for Toulouse. I want to show him that not everyone thinks he's a freak. But we're supposed to walk single file and not talk. And let's face it: for once I'm not the class freak. That's a good thing. Right?

When we enter the music room, Mr. Weldon pounces on us, as usual.

"Take your seats at once!" he shouts, then dabs his face with his white handkerchief. The guy is always sweating. This is probably because: one, he is always worked up, and, two, he always wears long-sleeved white shirts buttoned up to his throat with a skinny black tie that swings like a pendulum as he dabs his face with his hanky. He also wears a black vest, and black pants, and shiny black ankle-high boots. No wonder he sweats.

"No monkey business!" he practically shouts. "That means you, Vitus! Stop your stomping. Sit down! No pushing, Garrett! The risers are quite dangerous! There is to be no pushing, *any*one! I am not in the mood for monkey business! Are you listening, Garrett? I hope so, because I am not fooling around today. Sit down and be completely qui—!"

He stops mid-word when he sees Toulouse.

"Why, who are you, kind sir? Aren't you a dapper young man!"

"Dapper!" Garrett laughs behind his hand.

Hubcap snickers.

"Quiet!" Mr. Weldon snaps, whirling on them. "Quiet or I will give you a *solo* to sing."

Garrett shuts his mouth. Hubcap, too. If there's anything they dislike more than Mr. Logwood singing, it's having to sing themselves.

Mr. Weldon returns to Toulouse. "What is your name, young man?"

Toulouse stares at Mr. Weldon, speechless. He bows.

Mr. Weldon laughs. "Such a young gentleman! I love this boy!" He returns the bow.

Garrett and Hubcap try to hold it in but fail. They burst into laughter.

"Think Time!" Mr. Weldon roars at them.

"Both of you! Go and think! It will do you a world of good!"

I like Mr. Weldon. He scares me a little with all the sweating and whirling and roaring, but he sees right through Garrett and Hubcap, and sets them straight.

"His name is Toulouse," I say. "He's from Quebec."

"Ah!" Mr. Weldon says, wagging his finger at the ceiling. "*Oui, oui!* So it's *Monsieur* Toulouse! *Enchanté!* A great pleasure to meet you, monsieur. And welcome! *Bienvenue!* Please, have a seat and we will begin our musical lesson for today, which I hope you will find to your liking!"

Toulouse bows again and sits down. Mr. Weldon has cheered him up. Nothing like being treated special to lift your spirits.

The past few weeks we've been working on songs for the holiday concert in December. I've never heard of any of the songs Mr. Weldon is making us perform. We have no normal holiday songs, like "Jingle Bells" or "Frosty the Snowman." One is in Latin and dates from the someteenth century. We just sing *"dona nobis pacem"* over and over and over. It means "give us peace."

Mr. Weldon stands in front of us, takes a deep breath, raises his arms, then signals for us to start. We sing the song all the way through, with him mouthing it and making all sorts of hand gestures that mean louder or softer or faster or slower.

"Not too bad," Mr. Weldon says afterward. "From the top again, but this time, everyone sing, please, and with feeling. Monsieur Toulouse, would you like to join us?"

Toulouse nods.

"Excellent!" Mr. Weldon says. "And Garrett and Vitus, please return to the group, and please comport yourself like gentlemen."

They walk over and step up onto the risers without stomping.

We sing the song again.

"Bravo!" Mr. Weldon says. "Much better! And Toulouse, you sing like a bird."

I was thinking a flute, but his singing is kind of birdlike.

"A cuckoo," Garrett whispers to Hubcap, who snickers.

"Out!" Mr. Weldon says. "Out of my classroom. Go to the office, both of you. Such insolence!"

Mr. Weldon gets teased more than any of our teachers, but, like Toulouse, he doesn't seem to care much. He's a busy guy and can't spend all his energy trying to make everyone happy, or trying to be cool. Some teachers do that. They say "awesome" and give high fives. But Mr. Weldon doesn't pretend to be something he isn't.

Trying to be something you aren't is such a drag. What if you don't like making fun of people and threatening them and getting into trouble, like Garrett and Hubcap do? What if you like singing in Latin and making dragonfly lures and wearing a tie? Why can't you do what you want to do, be what you want to be?

Yeah, I like singing *"Dona Nobis Pacem."* I think it's cool to sing a song in an ancient language about peace. What's wrong with peace? I wish Garrett and Hubcap would leave me in peace. *Dona nobis pacem, dona nobis pacem.* I like peace.

I'm glad Mr. Weldon sent them to the office. Is that mean?

13. On Surviving Day One

On the way back to our class, the other kids start talking about Toulouse.

Monique: "Did you hear him sing?"

Ursula: "You call that singing? Mr. Weldon's right: he sounds like a bird."

Hubcap: "He's Mr. Weldon's new pet, that's for sure."

Garrett: "His pet weirdo, you mean."

Hubcap: "Yeah! His pet weirdo!"

Ursula: "I still want to know what happened to Otto."

Monique: "The way Toulouse stared at him was creepy."

She stops to squirt some hand sanitizer into one hand. She keeps a bottle of the stuff in her shoulder bag.

Ursula: "*So* creepy."

Garrett: "Totally. He's a freak."

Hubcap: "Totally."

Me: "Will you guys . . . why don't you . . . shut up?"

They all freeze. They don't expect this from me. Neither do I. It's one thing, though, when people say mean things about you. It's another when they say mean things about someone else. Especially someone nice like Toulouse. I can't imagine him saying mean things to anybody.

Before Garrett can get over his shock and shoot back an insult, Mr. Logwood comes over.

"Did I hear a disrespectful remark over here?" he asks.

"Yes, Mr. Logwood," Garrett says. "It was Woodrow. He told us to shut up."

I scowl at him. One of the rules at school— the *kid* rules—is that kids don't tell on other kids. If a kid does something against the adult rules, even if it's a kid you don't like, even if what he did is really bad, or even evil, it's against the rules to tell the adults.

The adults have to find out stuff on their own.

If I made the kid rules, I would get rid of this one. But I definitely don't make the rules. Kids like Garrett do.

However, another kid rule is that the kids who make the rules can break them whenever they feel like it. When you do as many mean things as Garrett does, you don't want other people telling on you. But he's allowed to tell, even on kids who didn't do anything wrong, even if he has to lie. He makes the rules, then he bends them or even breaks them whenever he feels like it.

"Woodrow?" Mr. Logwood asks, looking surprised. "Is this true?"

"They said . . . they were saying . . . mean things . . . about Toulouse."

This is the truth, but saying it is against the kid rules. No matter what I answered, I was in trouble here.

Garrett acts offended, but what he really is, is angry. He scowls at me. "That is not true, Mr. Logwood."

"Totally not true," Hubcap says.

Monique and Ursula look away. They're obeying the kid rules.

Mr. Logwood looks at all of us, one at a time. I can tell he believes me.

"Respect, students," he says. "Do I need to sing it?"

We all shake our heads. None of us want that.

14. Willow

I thought Toulouse would want to rush home after school. But he nodded when I invited him to go fishing, so we stopped at the office and called his house to get permission for him to get off at my stop. The secretary, Ms. Plowright, did the calling. She got the okay from Toulouse's mom, and he rode the bus home with me.

I guess this officially makes us friends. After telling Garrett to stop teasing him, I didn't really see any way around it. It was obvious to everybody that Toulouse and I were becoming friends. "Freaks of a feather flock together"— that's what Garrett said when Toulouse and I walked down the hall together to the office. I guess he's right.

My little sister, Willow, was a real pain on the ride home, pestering Toulouse with a billion questions.

"Why do you wear a suit like a grown-up?"

"Why do you wear a tie like one?"

"Why is your nose so pointy?"

"Why do you carry that instead of a backpack?"

"Where are you from?"

"Where do you live now?"

"Do you like it here?"

"Do you have a sister?"

"Why are you coming to our house?"

"Why do you keep staring at me like that?"

"Why won't you answer my questions?"

Mom's car wasn't in the driveway as my bus neared our stop. Usually she's home when Willow and I get there. Sometimes, though, she's still out on a job. My mom is a tree surgeon.

Dad's car is in the driveway. He's home, but he's probably sleeping, and we're supposed to be careful not to wake him. My dad works nights. He's a night watchman at a business park.

We go into the house and have a snack. I'm glad my mom isn't home. I want to show Toulouse around myself.

"We're going to my room," I tell Willow. "Do something quiet till Mom gets home. Dad's asleep."

"I *know*," she says with a scowl. "I'll play Librarian."

Librarian is a game she plays by herself. She checks books out to her stuffed animals, then she charges them fines when they don't return them on time. Like a stuffed animal could return a book.

Toulouse stands in the center of my room, holding his briefcase, looking as if he's waiting for me to say something, or maybe for a train in an old movie.

"Can I take your hat and coat?" I ask, just like Mr. Logwood did, only not as slowly.

Toulouse answers, "No, thank you."

He looks around at the stuff in my room, taking it in with his enormous eyes. He looks really interested, and suddenly I feel a little embarrassed. I haven't had a friend in here in a long, long time. Not since Farley Wopat, and that was in second grade. (Farley and his family moved away a few months later.) What does my room say about me?

It probably says I read a lot, but that I don't take such good care of my books. I rarely put them away. I stack them up like blocks and use them for stools, tables, and shelves. I leave them lying open, facedown, on the floor. I spill food and drink on them.

It probably also says that I like fiction, but that I read a lot of nonfiction, too. Books about fishing, rocketry, snakes, cryptids, weapons, raptors, semaphore, presidents, and lots of other things are mixed into the piles.

Visitors would also learn that I like duck tape. I keep a healthy supply of the stuff, in all sizes, colors, and patterns—including tie-dye, plaid, zebra, camo, mustache, penguin, zigzag, and candy corn—and I've created all sorts of things with it, including my lampshade, a few pillows, a couple of rugs, and a scratching post for our cats, Ouch and Meanie. Both cats were named by Willow, by the way, and both enjoy sharpening their claws on things made of duck tape. I made a duck tape scratching post hoping they'd leave my stuff alone. Instead, they leave the scratching post alone.

I guess my room also says I have cats. Cats who love duck tape.

"We have cats," I tell Toulouse, in case he's allergic. Lots of kids are.

He jumps.

"Don't worry," I say. "They're pretty harmless."

He starts trembling. Which makes me jittery. He looks nervously from side to side, by which I mean he swivels his head nervously from side to side. His shoulders don't budge.

"I m-mean, they hiss and swat, but they . . . they don't . . . you know . . . *injure* anybody or anything."

They do draw blood sometimes, but I don't tell Toulouse that.

"This is some stuff I found," I say, trying to change the subject. I walk over to my dresser, which is where I usually empty my pockets. I think of the pile as my midden, which is what a pack rat's stash is called. I'm proud of my stash, even if my parents and sister don't approve.

Toulouse approaches and looks it over carefully. Very carefully. He seems as interested in studying my jars of pebbles, glass shards, foil, wire, and other junk as he would be studying an encyclopedia, or an atlas, or a bowl of fish. In fact, he looks at it for so long that I start to wonder if we're going to do anything else this afternoon.

At least he's not freaked out about the cats anymore.

A knock on the door snaps him out of his trance. My mom steps in, wearing dirty brown work pants and a dirty denim work shirt. She's already taken off her tool belt, which is too bad. I'd like Toulouse to see her tools. My mom has good stuff.

15. Lynn

"Hey, Woodman," my mom says. Unlike Garrett's nickname, this is one I like, especially the "man" part. "Who's your little . . ." She stops when she sees how truly little Toulouse is. "Who's your friend?"

Mom knows enough not to interrogate Toulouse. She knows he and I are hanging out and to leave us alone. That's part of why she's such a great mom.

I tell her his name, and she says, "Nice meeting you, Toulouse. I'm Lynn. If you guys need anything, let me know," and leaves.

She wouldn't have gotten much info out of him anyway.

"Let's make some lures," I say.

He nods.

I like making lures. Flies, spinners, jigs—it doesn't matter. It feels good making things with my hands, including little things that require small motor skills and manual dexterity. We don't do things like that at school.

I get out my tackle box, which is an old steel lunch pail my dad found for me at a yard sale, and Toulouse takes his tackle box out of his briefcase. I have a vise attached to my drawing table for making lures, and, fortunately, I have a spare, so I attach it next to mine. Vises hold the lures securely while you work on them. Toulouse seems to know what I'm doing. I bet he has a vise at home. We get to work, stringing up some line, tying it off, then attaching things that will attract fish.

Certain fish like shiny things, and some like particular colors, or combinations of colors. Perch, in my experience, like purple, I've found. Croppies like feathers. Most of the fish I catch are sunfish, and they're not too fussy. They'll take about anything. After I catch them, though, I throw them back; they're too small.

When we've both made some lures, I go to

my closet to get a couple of rods. I have five or so, though I'm not sure where they all are. I give Toulouse the better one of the two. It has a reel that works. I also dig out two creels, which are little baskets to hold any fish we catch that are big enough to keep. Then we head out.

"We're going to the creek to fish," I tell my mom, who's stretched out on the couch with her laptop, studying a colorful table of words and numbers. Doing spreadsheets is part of a tree surgeon's job, too.

She checks her watch. "Okay, but don't be too long. It's getting dark earlier now." She looks at Toulouse. "Your parents picking you up or am I taking you home?"

"I will walk," he says in his hooty, breathy little voice.

He must like my mom to speak to her soon.

"Live nearby?" she asks.

I want to know this, too.

"Beyond the wood," he says. The last word goes on a while: "wooood."

I usually call it "the woods," but I like it without the *s*. It sounds fairy-taley.

Ouch saunters by and fires Toulouse a teeth-bared hiss.

Toulouse hops up onto a chair.

"Oh, Ouch," Willow says, waving him away. "Leave Toulouse alone. Sorry, Toulouse."

He gives her a nervous bow from the chair.

The cat hunkers off, his head low, glaring back at Toulouse.

"His parents know he's here, of course," Mom says to me, her eyebrows adding, *Right?*

"Uh-huh," I say.

"Then have fun. Catch me a whopper."

"Can I come with?" Willow asks. "I don't like to fish, but I can watch."

"No," I say.

She pouts. I look at Mom.

"We'll have fun here," she says to Willow.

"Want to play Librarian?" Willow asks.

"Sure," Mom answers, and smiles at me.

"Let's go," I say to Toulouse.

He hops down from the chair, gives my mom a bow, and we leave.

The wood (no *s*) is a few blocks away, past an open field. We don't live in town, but we don't live out of it, either. Kind of in between. We have neighbors, but their houses are far apart. Some of our neighbors have big gardens, or orchards, or fields with crops. One has a horse paddock. I often hear their horses whinny. I find lots of treasure for my midden in my neighborhood.

But today I'm not focusing on treasure. I'm focused on having company. Company *my age*, that is. Willow comes out with me sometimes, but that's different. She may be the same size as Toulouse, but she's not our age. I like having a friend over.

16. Out Here

When Toulouse and I enter the wood, the sun is low and shining at us like a giant motorcycle headlight through the trees. Mom's right: it is getting dark earlier.

Toulouse walks with his head tilted back, gazing up at the branches and the sky. He breathes in deeply and lets it out slowly. He's relaxed. I feel the same way.

It's quiet except for the sound of our feet snapping fir needles and the occasional tweeting bird. It's the opposite of school. No voices. No bells. No screaming or taunting or even whispering, except the wind through the branches. No teachers, no tests, no white-boards, no assignments, no walking single file. No Garrett. No Hubcap. Out here,

Toulouse and I aren't freaks. We fit in.

There aren't many bugs around the creek. It's too late in the year. Too cold. The water's high because it's been raining a lot. It's not roaring or anything—it's a small creek—but it's about as full as it ever gets.

Toulouse is good at casting. Casting isn't all that important on a creek this size, but it's fun to do, and I can tell he likes doing it. He gets a good swirl of line over his head, then, with a flick of his wrist, his hook, lure, and sinker shoot out over the water, then drop—*ploop!*

I stand upstream from him, giving him room, taking room for myself. A fisherman needs his own waters to fish. I make the first catch, a little sunfish, three or four inches long—too little to keep, too big for bait. I unhook it and throw it back. I glance over at Toulouse. He's staring at me as if he's shocked I threw the fish back.

He catches the next fish, and turns his body away as he unhooks it. I don't see him throw it back. I don't hear a *ploop!* I guess it must have been big enough to keep, and he tucked it into his creel.

I turn away and watch my line and listen to the creek gurgle. I read a biography of Isaac Newton once, partly because everybody had to read a biography for school, and partly because Isaac Newton happens to be one of my dad's heroes. The book said when Isaac was a kid he liked fooling around in creeks, and he grew up to be one of the most famous scientists ever. So there must be something good about fooling around in creeks, right?

Toulouse seems happy, too. He's a natural fisherman. Skillful. Calm. Patient. He's also a skillful, calm, patient painter, writer, and mathematician. How many kids do I know who would make the extra effort of not only writing with a quill and ink, but who would go to the bother of carrying that stuff around also? Not to mention an easel. And fishing tackle. Nobody I know.

Toulouse slips his hand into his coat and pulls out his pocket watch. He flips it open with a smooth motion, glances at it, then looks at me, frowning.

It's already time to head home.

We both sigh and start reeling in our lines. He finishes first and walks toward me.

"Where's your house from here?" I ask.

He points across the creek.

"How will you get across?"

Just then my hook snags the sleeve of my jacket. When I unhook it, it snags on my other sleeve. When I get it loose again and secure it to my reel, I look up and Toulouse is standing on the other side of the creek. He tips his hat, turns, and disappears into the trees.

I stand staring after him for quite a while, thinking. Then I notice that it's suddenly getting dark really quickly, so I start heading home.

Hoo! Hoo! a bird says in a flutish voice from somewhere.

I love the wood.

17. Weird Is Normal

"He's cute in his little suit," Willow says at dinner. "Hey, I rhymed! I'm a poet and don't know it!"

"Yes, you do," I say. "You just said you were."

She makes a sad face. "Oh."

"Toulouse is an artist, and he's also the smartest," I say.

"You're a poet and don't know it, too!"

"No, I know it."

"Wish I'd gotten the chance to meet him," Dad says.

Dad always wakes up in time for dinner. He'll leave for work at the business park after I'm asleep, and will be home and awake when I get up for school. It must be strange to be nocturnal.

Dad wears thick glasses with fragile-looking

wire frames. The frames are always bent, so his glasses always sit crooked on his face. Dad's balding on top and has a bushy mustache and adult braces on his teeth. He wears a tie without a jacket and a white, button-up, short-sleeved shirt. It's easy to imagine him as a science nerd when he was a kid.

Which he says he was. My dad loves science. He reads a lot of books about it, which is probably why I read so much nonfiction. He says he's always been a science nerd and often got teased about it when he was growing up. He also liked to stick things he found in his pockets. He still does.

He didn't become a scientist, though, because his family didn't have enough money to send him to college, and his grades weren't good enough to earn him scholarships. But he has always studied on his own. Being a night watchman gives him plenty of time to read. He calls himself an autodidact, a person who teaches himself, like Isaac Newton did. He says people probably used to call Isaac a science nerd, too—though, because he lived so long ago, probably not in those words.

"He was so little, Poppy," Willow says. "Littler than me!"

"That's not his fault," I say.

"No, if he could, I bet he'd be big like me. Everyone wants to be big."

Willow's pretty bubbly and talkative like this most of the time. It's cute, but sometimes it gets old.

"His hat was *adorable*!" she says.

"A bowler," Mom says to Dad.

"And he's from Quebec, eh?" Dad says. "Does he speak French or English? Or both?"

"He doesn't speak much at all," I say. "But he's spoken some French words and some English. And he seems to understand English pretty well. He had a French/English dictionary in his briefcase, and a quill and a bottle of ink, which is what he writes with. He loves fishing. And he makes lures. He keeps tackle in his briefcase, too."

"Sounds like your kind of kid," Mom says.

"The kids calls him weird. And odd."

"Weird *and* odd, eh?" Dad says with a laugh.

"And they made fun of him for being little."

"He *is* little," Willow says. "*So* little!"

That's what I mean about the cute stuff getting old.

"It's lucky he befriended you on his first day then, isn't it?" Mom says.

Mom is kind of weird, too, I guess, in her lumberjack clothes, and with her muscly arms and neck and her red, outdoorsy face. She never wears perfume or makeup, or girly clothes. She hates shopping, in fact. She loves rock and roll and blasts it when she's driving in her beat-up old truck. Not all moms play air guitar when they drive, I bet. Mine does.

She's normal to me, though. So is Dad. Even Willow, the bubbly librarian. Maybe weird is normal.

"I was thinking of inviting him over Saturday to fish some more," I say.

"I wonder if he wears the same clothes on the weekend," my mom says.

Dad shrugs.

"I bet he does," Willow adds.

So do I.

18. Loyalty

Toulouse didn't wear the same clothes to school the next day. Well, he wore the same jacket, gloves, and shoes, but today's black pants have gray pinstripes, the vest is dark red instead of black, his tie has a diamond pattern, and, on his head, he's wearing a brilliant red bowler.

Despite how beautiful it is, the hat gets laughs, which I doubt is why he chose to wear it. I wonder if he thought twice about wearing it, if he figured out that his wardrobe doesn't match ours, that the kids are teasing him because of it, but decided to go ahead and wear the red hat anyway, because he likes it.

That was my thinking back when I wore my duck tape clothes. But after months of being teased, I finally gave up. The fun of wearing them was spoiled by the snickering and taunting. I surrendered.

I wonder if Toulouse will. I wonder if he'll still be wearing a suit a month from now. I hope so.

"Good morning, Toulouse," I say as he unpacks his ink bottle and quill.

He tips his red hat. I wish I had one to tip back. It's so dignified, tipping hats. But they're not allowed in class.

"That was fun yesterday, at the creek."

He bows again.

"I was thinking we could go again, tomorrow, if you're free."

Tomorrow's Saturday.

"Are you guys dating?" Garrett interrupts.

Hubcap: "Yeah! You two going out?"

"We're *ten*," I say.

I glance at Toulouse, double-checking with my eyes. He nods. He's ten.

"So it's a *play*date," Garrett says.

Hubcap: "Yeah!"

"We're going fishing," I say, though I really

should ignore them. Like Toulouse does.

There's a beep, and the principal's voice comes out of the speaker. Saved by the morning announcements.

"Good morning, students. This is Principal McDowell. Please stand for the pledge."

We all stand and lay our hands on our hearts. Toulouse seems unsure about the hand-on-heart thing. Maybe they don't have to pledge allegiance in Quebec. He does lay his hand on his chest, but he doesn't recite the pledge with us. I doubt he knows the words. I don't even listen to what I'm saying when I say them.

"'. . . andtotherepublic . . . forwhichitstands . . .'"

The pledge ends. The principal introduces the two students who have been reading the announcements this month. I don't know them. William something and Olivia something. They're fifth graders.

"Photographers will be here today for Picture Make-Up Day," Olivia says, "for those of you who missed Picture Day in September."

And for those of us who lived in Quebec in September . . .

I glance at Toulouse. His eyes are opened very wide. They're as big as Oreos. He looks worried, bordering on scared. He must not like having his picture taken.

I know how he feels. "Smile," they say, but no one can. We grin instead. Grinning isn't smiling. When you grin you're either faking it or up to something.

I peek at Garrett. He grins at me. So does Hubcap.

Toulouse coughs. He coughs harder. He hacks. He's gagging on something.

I tap him on the back, swiftly but not hard. He keeps gagging.

"He's choking!" Ursula says. "During announcements! I can't *hear*!"

"Give him the Heimlich!" Monique says.

I stand up and wrap my arms around him, grip my left wrist with my right hand, and pull.

"*Hoof!*" Toulouse says.

Everyone shrieks. I hear something land on his desk. I'm behind him, so I can't see it.

Everyone sticks out their tongues in disgust. Whatever he coughed up is grossing them out. I step around.

The thing on his desk is about the size of a golf ball. It's dark brown, like dirt, and has fur. It's a dirt clod with fur.

And it came out of Toulouse.

19. Okay

I walk with Toulouse to the office, to see the nurse, as Mr. Logwood instructed. He also instructed me to ask that a janitor be sent to our classroom, and he instructed me to hurry—though we were not to run in the halls.

Before I left the room, I saw him use a paper towel to pick up the thing that Toulouse upchucked and seal it in a plastic sandwich bag. Maybe Mr. Logwood intends to have it analyzed. If so, I wouldn't mind seeing the results.

"I'm sorry you threw . . . you don't feel well," I whisper to Toulouse as we walk briskly down the halls.

He doesn't reply.

I'd like to ask what he ate for breakfast

this morning but decide it's too personal a question, and, most likely, rude.

"I am okay," he answers in a tiny voice.

"*Now*, you mean," I say. "I often feel better after . . . you know . . . after I vomit."

He nods.

At the nurse's station, I say, "Wait there . . . on that chair . . . for Edward . . . He'll take care of you. He's our nurse. I have to go talk to Ms. . . . the secretary."

"I am okay," he says again.

"Tell that to Edward . . . and don't worry . . . he's nice. He'll probably give you a mint for . . . for the taste. I'll see you back in the classroom. Edward will bring you there when he's done with you . . . after he's sure you're okay . . . which I'm sure you are."

"I am okay," he says for the third time.

"Right. So everything will be fine." I try to smile, which means I grin, then I walk away.

I tell Ms. Plowright that Mr. Logwood wants a janitor to come to our room to clean up a mess that a sick student made, and she picks up the phone.

In the hall on the way back, I think about how everyone will laser-beam poor Toulouse when he gets back to class. They'll melt his skin and bones and heart with their eyes. He'll be defenseless against them.

At least that's what it feels like to me after I do something stupid and get sent to the office. When I jammed the chopsticks down my throat, for example. And when I accidentally choked on a scented dry-erase marker. They make them smell too good.

I want to protect Toulouse, but how can I when I can't even protect myself?

I think about this as I walk through the halls, and come up with a plan that might work.

20. Works Like a Charm

I walk through the door. It's Read-Aloud. Mr. Logwood is sitting in his armchair in the Gathering Place, holding the book we've been reading, *Poppy*.

Hubcap, who can never focus during Read-Aloud, sees me first. He elbows Garrett, who swats at him. Garrett loves Read-Aloud. He gets completely absorbed in the stories and dislikes distractions to the point of hitting anyone who bothers him. When Hubcap elbows him again, Garrett shoots him a this-better-be-worth-it look. Hubcap makes a hitchhiker gesture toward me. Garrett glances over, and his face lights up. It's worth it.

Other kids sense that something is going on behind them and twist around. Within moments, I have the attention of the entire class. As planned.

On the way back from the office I stopped in the boys' bathroom and made a quick duck-tape bow tie and bowler. The hat is neon green. The bow tie is made of a duck tape with a mustache print. Those are the two tapes I happen to have in my pockets today.

The idea was that I'd attract the class's teasing away from Toulouse and onto me. And it's working like a charm.

"Is it Halloween already?" Garrett asks.

Hubcap: "Yeah, nice costume, Woody."

"That's enough," Mr. Logwood says, though he seems to be fighting snickers himself. "Or shall I break into song?"

Everyone shuts up.

"Maybe you'd like to hang up your hat, Woodrow," Mr. Logwood says to me.

"No, I'd like"—my throat closes up—"to keep it . . . on?" This last word I squeak.

"Like his *boy*friend," Hubcap says.

"Please take a Think Time, Vitus," Mr. Logwood says.

Hubcap stands and stomps away.

"Please, Woodrow," Mr. Logwood says. "As you know, wearing hats is not allowed in the building."

"You let Tou . . . Toulouse," I say.

"Yeah! If Toulouse can, why can't Woodrow?" Monique asks.

"It's only fair," Ursula says.

"Yeah!" Garrett says. Which surprises me—and everyone else. As a rule, Garrett does not stand up for me. Or anyone, except himself.

"Quiet, please," Mr. Logwood says. "This is Read-Aloud, which is intended as a quiet, listening time. If you do not wish to quietly listen, you can return to your desk and write a summary of the book so far."

Total silence, like someone hit the Mute button.

"Woodrow, I've been allowing Toulouse to wear his hat in class because he is new not only to this school, but to the United States, and I thought it best he be allowed to hold on to something that clearly gives him comfort during what must be a challenging transition.

In time, I'll ask him to comply with school rules. You, on the other hand, having attended Uwila since kindergarten, must certainly be used to our conventions and rules. I expect you to comply with them now."

He makes a good point. It's obvious from all the nodding that everyone agrees with it. I didn't think this all the way through. I got the attention I was after. I should have left it at that. I should have taken the hat off when he asked. Now my face is burning, and I feel as if I'm going to faint.

I remove my hat, then fumble with it, and end up dropping it. When I bend over to pick it up, stuff from my pockets spills out onto the floor with a clatter.

The snickering returns. I hope it lasts till Toulouse gets back, and he can slip in without notice.

21. Lenny the Magnet Boy

He doesn't return while I'm picking up my stuff.

He doesn't return during Read-Aloud.

He doesn't return by Writing Workshop, and I was hoping to do some peer editing with him on my story "Lenny the Magnet Boy," which is about a kid who gets magnetized after fooling around with his dad's metal detector. Forks and fish hooks and other metal stuff start flying at him. He ends up stuck to the refrigerator. I haven't come up with a decent ending yet, and I was hoping maybe Toulouse would have an idea.

Instead, I get paired up with Monique. It could be worse. It could be Ursula. Or Garrett.

Or Hubcap. Monique can actually be kind of nice. She says the story is funny, but she thinks some of the objects that fly at him would be too heavy. The hammers, for example.

"Good point," I say.

"But the hammers are funny," she says. "Maybe Lenny becomes a really, really strong magnet. Then he could attract something that he could use to pry himself off the fridge. Like a crowbar."

"Not bad," I say. "Not bad at all."

Monique's story is about a twelve-year-old girl named Natasha who finds out her mom and dad aren't her real parents, so she sets out to find them. She discovers they live in Paris and flies there to look for them.

"Alone?" I ask.

"Yes. She's very brave."

"But can kids . . . like . . . can they fly by themselves? I mean, don't you . . . don't they . . . have to have an adult . . . like a parent . . . with you . . . them?"

"My cousin flew here last summer by herself, and she's twelve."

"But I bet she had to have her parents' . . . Her parents probably had to fill out . . . you know . . . *forms*. And take her . . . to the airport."

She thinks about this.

"And Natasha . . . she's flying overseas," I say. "Wouldn't she . . . will she need a passport . . . or something?"

Monique thinks awhile longer, then says, "Maybe she finds out her parents live in the same town she lives in."

"Good idea, but not as exciting."

We start revising.

Toulouse isn't back by recess. I'm worried about him. Maybe Edward found something bad. Maybe Toulouse is very sick. I mean, who throws up things like that?

Music comes after recess on Fridays. Mr. Weldon teaches it. He does both music and choir, which makes sense.

Music class is different than choir, though. We don't sing. We play instruments. But not till after we've learned something about music. Today we learn about rests.

Some rests are one beat. Some are more.

Each one has a different symbol. They can be combined if the composer wants the musicians to pause for a length of time that doesn't have its own symbol. Six beats, for example, is a four-beat rest (called a whole rest) plus a two-beat rest (a half rest). Music is kind of like math, except you can hear it.

After we learn about rests, we practice, first by counting out loud as Mr. Weldon points at the written music on the overhead. Then we clap it. Finally, we get to use instruments. Everybody loves getting to use the instruments. Kids love making noise.

We usually don't get to use the instruments for long, though. Somebody always ends up banging on one of them too loud, or wielding one like a weapon, and then Mr. Weldon takes them away. It doesn't seem fair, especially with a kid like Hubcap in our class. A guy like him is always going to mess things up for everyone.

I like playing the castanets, which are tiny finger cymbals. If I were Lenny the magnet boy, I could suck them right to my hand. But I'm not, and I have to wait for my turn to choose an instrument. Unfortunately, Hubcap goes before me, and he knows I like the castanets, so he takes them. He doesn't even like them; he likes the loud instruments, the ones you bang, like drums and wood blocks. But I guess he likes messing with me more.

I take a recorder, and right after I do, Toulouse walks in. I'm so glad he's back that I run over to him.

"No running in class," Garrett says.

Hubcap shouts, "Yeah, Woody—walk!"

Mr. Weldon gives Hubcap a Think Time for shouting.

Nobody says a word about what happened before, when Toulouse choked. They're all too busy with their instruments. I guess in the end, I didn't need to make the duck-tape hat and tie. But I don't regret it. How can I? I still have the hat and tie.

22. Ooh-LOW

"Monsieur!" Mr. Weldon exclaims, and claps his hands together, his fingers pointed upward. *"Bienvenue,* Toulouse! Welcome! I worried you weren't going to be with us today! Here, for you, something special!"

He unlocks his off-limits supply cabinet with the small silver key he keeps on a chain around his neck.

"Come here, Monsieur Hulot!" He pronounces it *ooh-LOW.*

Toulouse walks over and looks inside.

"Take whichever instrument you like," Mr. Weldon says.

Toulouse looks up at him, then back into the cabinet. He leans in and comes out with a small red plastic accordion. It looks like a toy, but then all the instruments Mr. Weldon gives us look like toys. Toulouse pulls open the accordion, and it wheezes. The bellows are blue and made of cardboard. Toulouse covers some of the accordion's little buttons with his fingers and squeezes. It wheezes again, but this time there's a tune in it.

"Ah, you *play*!" Mr. Weldon says. "Please, monsieur, regale us with a song!"

I guess Toulouse doesn't have to count or clap first.

He pulls the accordion open again, and then squeezes it shut, then opens it again. He does know how to play it. He plays a song. It's cheerful, but with a slight sadness to it. Toulouse shuts his eyes and sways slightly. He plays an entire song, from memory.

Everyone is silent, then Mr. Weldon starts slapping his hands together loudly and cheering, *"Magnifique! Bravo! Bravo, Monsieur Hulot!"*

We start to clap and cheer, too. Some do so because they'll do anything if it means they get to make noise, but a lot of us mean it. We're impressed. I don't know if there's anyone in our class who can play a whole song on an instrument as well as Toulouse just did.

Toulouse bows twice.

When the clapping winds down, Mr. Weldon says, "That was 'Reine de Musette,' no?"

Toulouse nods.

"A beautiful tune, played beautifully!" Mr. Weldon gushes. He actually has tears in his eyes.

Then Garrett says in a loud voice, "What was that thing you puked up on your desk, Toulouse?"

"Yeah!" Hubcap says. "And what did you do to Otto?"

Mr. Weldon gets mad and sends them to the office.

I'm mad, too, and not just because they brought up the two things I didn't want brought up. I'm mad at Garrett and Hubcap because they hated the fact that Toulouse was impressing everyone and getting attention, so they decided to spoil it. They intentionally tried to embarrass him. It's mean to try to knock somebody down just because they're flying higher than you. Falling hurts more the higher you are. I know this from personal experience.

Toulouse puts the accordion back in the cabinet.

"Oh, please, monsieur," Mr. Weldon says, "won't you please play us another song?"

Toulouse picks up a triangle and comes over and stands next to me.

"Have it your way, monsieur," Mr. Weldon says, pouting.

I lean over and whisper to Toulouse, "I'd sure like to sock both of those guys right on their noses."

He looks up at me.

"'Sock' means 'punch,'" I say.

He nods.

"You're really good at the accordion."

He tips his hat.

"Okay, everyone," Mr. Weldon says. "Ready? All together now: One . . . two . . . three . . . ready . . . begin!"

We bang and shake and toot our instruments, making a pretty awful noise. We smile.

23. Winding and Unwinding

I'm a picky eater, and none of the few foods I like—pizza, chicken nuggets, nachos—are being served today. Lunch is beef stew, which smells weird and has green peppers, which I don't eat. The side dishes are not tater tots or french fries or even mashed potatoes, but steamed carrots and cole slaw. The dessert is red Jell-O. I may starve.

I fish out some beef chunks and slurp up the Jell-O, then dump my tray into the trash and head outside. Toulouse is up in his tree.

"How do you get up there?" I yell.

He stares at me a long time, then shrugs.

"I'll be right back."

I walk around, scanning the playground

for something to drag over and climb on, though I know there isn't anything. The adults have removed everything a kid could make something fun out of, or use as a weapon. All I find on the playground are kids, a recess teacher, some balls (which are, at the moment, being used by Garrett and Hubcap as weapons), and heavy play equipment sunk in concrete.

I turn around and trip over Toulouse.

"How do you do that?" I ask, helping him up and dusting him off.

He makes a hacking cough and a puff of dust comes out his mouth.

I'm relieved that it's only dust.

"You want to swing?" I ask. I see that two swings next to each other have opened up, a rare occurrence.

Toulouse picks up his briefcase, dusts it off, coughs again, then nods.

I take off running, yelling, "Dibs on the swings! Dibs on the swings! *Oof!*" I trip and fall on my face. And on a couple of rolls of duck tape, a compass, and my steel pencil sharpener, all of which are in my front pockets. Ouch.

No way will we get the swings now. I climb to my feet and look back at Toulouse.

He's not there.

I look at the swing set. There he is, perched on a swing, holding the chain of the one next to it.

"You can't save swings," Ursula says to him, her arms crossed angrily.

Toulouse stares at her.

I run over and dive at the swing. I land on it on my stomach. My momentum sends the swing back and up; it twists, then unwinds as it swings back down. I get dizzy, lose my balance, and fall off.

Ursula catches my swing and sits on it.

Toulouse hops off his and helps me up.

"Get out of the way!" Ursula yells at us.

Toulouse turns his head toward her and stares.

"Do it," she growls. "Move! Move now! Move, you little freak!"

"Respect," he says in his flutey voice.

24. Lion Eats Most of Boy

Toulouse shows me a story in another one of his old books. The book is called *Cautionary Tales for Children* and the story's title is "Jim, Who Ran Away from His Nurse and Was Eaten by a Lion"—which is a spoiler, if you ask me. The lion doesn't eat all of Jim. It doesn't get to his head, but only because the zookeeper comes along before it can. It doesn't seem fair to me that the lion eats Jim. All he did wrong was wander away from his nurse in a crowd. Getting eaten by a lion for wandering off seems harsh.

Strange that Toulouse showed me this story. Maybe he's a little angry at Ursula?

Next he shows me a story called "Godolphin Horne, Who Was Cursed with the Sin of Pride, and Became a Boot-Black." Godolphin is smug and rude. He doesn't shake hands and always smirks. He gets a chance to work as a page for the court, but, because he's so nasty, the king and a duchess and some bishops all say they don't want him. So Godolphin gets fired and becomes a poor shoeshine boy.

I think Toulouse is angry at Garrett, too.

When I finish it, I glance up at Toulouse and he has to cover his mouth to hide his laughter.

"Well, look at the worms," Garrett says from below us. We're sitting on the Ladder to Nowhere.

Hubcap: "Yeah, worms!"

"Worms?" Toulouse whispers to me. He seems scared. Or is he excited? It's hard to tell with his huge eyes.

"He means 'bookworms,'" I say. "It's what people who don't read call people who do."

It doesn't make sense that Garrett, who likes Read-Aloud so much, would make fun of reading. But then Garrett rarely makes sense.

"Who reads books on a playground?" Garrett asks, though it's not a question. He can see who does.

"Freaky bookworms!" Hubcap says.

"Worms," Toulouse says again, and licks his lips. He sure has a pointy mouth. It comes out at the center when he talks. Maybe it's because he grew up speaking French. People who speak French speak with real puckery lips. At least they do in movies. I haven't met anyone who speaks French except Toulouse and Mr. Weldon, and they both speak with puckery lips.

"What did you call us?" Garrett snarls.

Hubcap: "Did you just call us worms?"

"That's not . . . he didn't . . . ," I say.

"Why don't you come down here and say that?" Garrett says.

Hubcap: "Yeah!"

"He was . . . he just said . . . you know . . . he was *repeating* . . ."

"Just get down here, you chicken!" Garrett says.

Hubcap: "Bluck, bluck!"

"Chicken?" Toulouse says. Again, he licks his lips. Is he hungry?

"It's another expression," I whisper. "He's calling us scaredy-cats."

"*Cats?*"

This time he definitely looks scared.

"That's right, they're scaredy-cats," Garrett says, and elbows Hubcap.

Hubcap: "Yeah! Scaredy-cats! Meow, me— *Oof!*"

Toulouse lands on Hubcap's chest, knocking him flat on his back on the ground. Hubcap is stunned. Garrett is stunned. I'm stunned.

Toulouse stares deeply into Hubcap's wide eyes. Waiting for him—daring him?—to speak.

"I . . . I . . . I . . . ," Hubcap stammers.

"Not cats," Toulouse says to him, leaning in close. "No. *Cats.*"

I wait for Garrett to jump in and help Hubcap, but he doesn't. He just stands there with his mouth moving like he's talking, but nothing comes out.

It's nice to see both of them speechless for once.

The bell rings. Saved again. It's not a coincidence. Recesses are just really short.

Toulouse hops off Hubcap. Garrett rushes to his henchman and helps him to his feet.

"We'll take care of them later," he snarls.

Hubcap: "Yeah. Later."

They hurry away toward the building, glancing nervously back at us over their shoulders.

I'm still on the Ladder. I tuck Toulouse's book into his briefcase and click it shut. Suddenly, he's sitting next to me.

"Wow" is all I can think of to say.

He shakes his head. "No cats."

25. Our Zone

Toulouse enters a stall in the boy's locker room carrying a long gray duffel, then exits half a minute later wearing a baggy gray sweatsuit, black high-tops, and a red stocking cap. He's still wearing his gloves.

Garrett snickers and nudges Hubcap.

"Toulouse the athlete," Garrett says.

Hubcap: "Yeah!"

I'm tempted to point out how Toulouse just flattened Hubcap on the playground but decide to leave it alone. I'd probably just stutter anyway.

We're playing volleyball in P.E. this week. Ms. Otwell divides us into two teams. I volunteer to sit out the first game when it turns out the class is uneven. I pretend to be crushed as I walk toward the bleachers, but I don't mind at all. I avoid competitive sports whenever I can. I don't like them, and I'm clumsy, which gives Garrett and Hubcap more to taunt me about.

Toulouse follows me to the bleachers.

Everyone watches him. Garrett and Hubcap, of course, snicker.

"It's okay," I whisper to Toulouse. "Go on and play. Have fun."

He stays where he is.

Ms. Otwell comes over. "I have an idea, Woodrow. Why don't you and your new friend *share* a position."

How did she know Toulouse is my new friend?

"Yeah," Garrett says. "Put them together and you might make one whole player!"

Hubcap: "One who stinks!"

They both get warnings from Ms. Otwell. One more disrespectful outburst and they will sit out the game.

Toulouse and I take our position on the court, and the game begins. We're on the same team with Garrett and Hubcap, and they keep stepping in front of us to hit balls coming our way.

"Hit only the balls that come to your zone!" Ms. Otwell orders.

Garrett and Hubcap obey.

I don't know if volleyball is big in Quebec, but Toulouse seems pretty experienced at it. He easily returns the ball hit to us, though usually he sets up other players rather than hitting the ball back over. When someone sets him up, he leaps up and spikes. For such a little guy, he really gets off the ground. This could explain how he's able to get up and down from his tree and the Ladder and the swing set so fast, but it doesn't explain how he got across the creek. The creek is way too wide to jump across.

When our turn to serve comes, Toulouse aces it. Everyone stands there, gaping. Some people clap and cheer.

Is the kid good at everything?

Garrett and Hubcap aren't clapping or cheering. They are fuming. They have also noticed that I'm not exactly participating. I've been letting Toulouse hit all the balls that come to our zone.

"Hey, Woody!" Garrett says. "Can I get you a chair?"

Hubcap: "Yeah, Woody! Don't *do* something. Just *stand* there!"

Ms. Otwell gives them another warning. One more and they'll have to sit out the game.

Ms. Otwell doesn't always stick to her guns.

Toulouse holds the ball out to me. It sure looks huge in his hands. You can't even see his face.

"*You* serve, Toulouse," I say. "You're good at it. I'm not."

"Who?" he asks.

"Me! You serve."

He won't. He just keeps offering me the ball.

"I think Toulouse is saying it's your turn to serve, Woodrow," Ms. Otwell says.

Everyone starts getting restless and grumbling at me, so I take the ball. I toss it in the air, punch at it, miss, then it lands on my head. Everybody but Toulouse and Ms. Otwell crack up. Garrett laughs so hard I hope he chokes.

"Will you *please* serve?" I ask Toulouse.

He shakes his head. The kid's stubborn.

"Okay then," I say. "Get ready for strike two."

I toss the ball again, but this time I manage to hit it—into the back of Monique's head.

"Hey!" she screeches.

The gym echoes with laughter.

"Side out!" Ms. Otwell calls.

As we change positions, Garrett sticks his foot out and trips me. I don't fall all the way to the floor. I just squawk like a parrot because I think I'm going to.

Ms. Otwell finally follows through. "Take a seat on the bleachers, Garrett, and stay quiet or I'll send you to the office."

Garrett glares at me, then stomps over to the bleachers.

"Woodrow, take his zone," Ms. Otwell orders.

Hubcap glares at me as I obey.

I do the best I can during the game, which isn't great, but I do sometimes manage to hit a ball up in the air instead of miss it, or punch it into the net, or into the ground, or into one of my teammates' heads.

Toulouse gives me encouraging smiles and nods whenever I look over at him. When I do particularly well, he claps.

I'm sort of enjoying myself.

In P.E.

Now that's weird.

26. Wink

People are different toward Toulouse after the game. Interested. Attentive. All because he was good at volleyball. That's what happens when you excel at competitive sports. Before that he was the weird freak in the weird clothes who maybe swallowed, then regurgitated our fish and definitely coughed up a furry golf ball. Now, he's fascinating. A star.

He's not crazy about it. After the game, he hides behind me as best he can. Then he disappears. A couple of minutes later, he walks out of the locker room, fully dressed.

When we're back in class, Monique comes up to me.

"Woodrow, can you make duck-tape bangles?"

"What?" I ask. I'm not sure she's talking to me. She doesn't usually ask me things out of the blue. Also, I'm not sure I know what bangles are.

"Can you make me some bangles out of duck tape." She shakes her arm, and her bracelets clink together.

"Oh, *bangles*," I say. "Sure . . . I guess . . . but they wouldn't . . . I don't think they would . . . duck tape doesn't . . . well . . . *clink*."

"Good point," she says seriously, and shakes her bangles again. "I need them to clink."

"Come on, Woody, can't you make them clink for her?" Garrett asks. "What kind of girl's-jewelry maker are you?"

Hubcap snickers.

I ignore him.

"They won't clink, but I could make . . . if you want one . . . I could make a . . . what do you call it? . . . A . . . one of those princessy crown things . . . if you . . . you know . . . want . . ."

She shakes her head. "I don't want a tiara."

"Right—a tiara. No, okay . . . how about a little purse thing? . . . maybe a wallet?" I pull out my duck-tape stash. "Like, a small bag with a flap . . . maybe Velcro? . . . for your hand sanitiz—"

I don't finish because I'm not sure I should be mentioning her hand sanitizer. She always has some with her, and it's never in the same bottle, like she has a collection. I'm not sure what it's all about, but I'm not judging. I'm sure she wonders about me and my duck tape. I know she does. She's made fun of me about it before. I don't want to make fun of her.

Monique has collected a lot of different things over the years. She used to love erasers, the kind you stick on the ends of pencils. She had a million of them. Then one day, no more erasers. Instead, she loved stickers. She stuck stickers on everything. Then, gone. Next it was buttons, the kind with pins on the back and sayings on the front, like YOU SAY POTATO, I SAY TATER TOT and I'M CORRECTING YOUR GRAMMAR IN MY MIND. Her jackets and her backpack were covered with them. Now it's bangles.

"Yeah," she says dreamily. "A clutch purse. I like clutches."

Maybe clutches will be her next thing. Maybe duck-tape clutches.

"Why don't you draw . . . you're a good . . . draw a picture of . . . you know . . . what you want? . . . And write down the colors you want . . . where you want them . . . and I'll . . . I can make it . . . easy."

"Well"—she says, ripping a piece of paper out of her notebook—"it should be a rectangle, of course . . ." And she draws one, then adds a triangular flap.

"Okay," I say. "I could make a hole? . . . For you to close it?" I draw a line across the flap. "It could . . . you know . . . tuck in. . . ."

She nods, and draws a second line. "Two slits. It could go in one and out the other. That would hold better."

"Good idea," I say. "Very . . . clever." My face feels hot.

"Thanks," she says.

"I can . . . I'll make it . . . as soon as I can."

"Okay, gang, let's line up," Mr. Logwood says. "A good day. Well done."

We line up to leave. I'm behind Ursula and

Toulouse. Toulouse turns his head all the way around and winks at me.

I wonder why.

Did he have something to do with Monique's request?

Maybe he's just letting me know he noticed that Monique was nice to me. Does he understand already how unusual that is?

Maybe the wink had nothing to with Monique. Maybe it was just a friendly wink. When it comes to people acting friendly toward me, I'm not the best judge. I'm a little rusty.

Maybe I'm overthinking this. I have a tendency to do that.

Maybe it was just a wink.

I wink back.

27. Little Weirdo

While we're waiting in line to leave, I overhear Garrett talking to Hubcap.

Garrett: "So the little freak can hit a volleyball. Big deal."

Hubcap: "Big deal."

Garrett: "I can hit a volleyball better than he can, but the teacher wouldn't let me play."

Hubcap: "Right. So unfair."

Garrett: "He's still a little weirdo."

Hubcap: "So weird."

Garrett: "A freak."

Hubcap: "Exactly. A weird little freak."

I look for Mr. Logwood, hope he's hearing this, but he's across the room at his desk, stapling together papers, probably for us to take home.

"Watch this," Garrett says.

Hubcap: "What are you going to do?"

"Just watch."

He walks up to Toulouse and me.

"Hey, Toulouse," he says. "Your shoe's untied."

Is he kidding? That's the oldest trick in the book. But before I can warn him, Toulouse tilts his head forward to look at his shoes, which, of course, are tied. Garrett quickly slaps the brim of Toulouse's red bowler and it sails up into the air.

While everyone else watches the hat twirling overhead, I watch Toulouse scoot under the nearest desk. He doesn't even have to duck. He peers out with terrified eyes.

I spring up and snatch the hat out of the air. I smoothly feed it to Toulouse under the desk, then turn to face Garrett. If blood boils, that's what mine is doing. Garrett has done a lot of mean things to me over the years, but I don't think any of them ever made me this mad.

"You . . . ," I say. That's the only word that comes out.

He covers his mouth and snickers. So does Hubcap. This makes me even madder.

"You . . . are . . ." Oh, dear. Is this going to come out one word at a time?

More snickering. Toulouse steps out from his hiding place, the hat back on his head, and stands beside me. This gives me courage. And purpose.

"Cruel," I finish. "You are cruel. From now on . . . from now *on* . . ."

I know what I want to say, but suddenly I'm aware everyone is listening, and the words get literally stuck in my throat. I can feel them down there, hiding like Toulouse under the desk, afraid to come out. Finally, my anger pushes them free.

"Leave . . . Toulouse . . . alone," I say. This time I'm not stammering. I'm speaking slowly and clearly, so that he can't misunderstand me. "And while you're at it, leave *me* alone, too."

"Yeah," Monique says. "Stop being a bully, Garrett."

"What'd I do?" he asks.

"You knocked his hat off," I say. "And you and Hubcap went through his briefcase. And you tried to trip me in gym." Boy, I'm on a roll. "And you called Toulouse names. Mean names. Like you call me. 'Freak.' 'Dork.' 'Worm.' And you tease us just because we're friends."

"Friends," Toulouse says.

"Right," I say, peeking down at him.

Hubcap snickers.

"You do it, too," I say to him. "You do every mean thing Garrett does, you little copycat."

"Cat?" Toulouse says.

"No," I whisper to him. "No cat."

Mr. Logwood finally comes over, and people back up to let him through.

"Everything okay over here?" he asks, looking at Garrett and Hubcap, then at Toulouse and me. "Woodrow? What's happening?"

I can't speak. I have a lot to say, but the words rush to my throat so fast they create a traffic jam.

"My shoes are tied, Garrett," Toulouse says.

Garrett can't help himself. He snickers. Hubcap, too.

"Garrett knocked Toulouse's hat off," I say. "And he called him names. Mean names. He's been doing it a lot."

"Is that true, Toulouse?" Mr. Logwood asks.

Toulouse's head pivots to Garrett. He blinks. I see those diagonal lines again. He pivots to Hubcap. He blinks. He's telling on them without telling.

"It *is* true, Mr. Logwood," Monique says.

Ursula nods. A lot of kids nod. I'm not the only one who's tired of Garrett's and Hubcap's meanness.

"What is a 'weirdo'?" Toulouse asks Mr. Logwood.

"All right, Garrett, Vitus, please go over to the Gathering Place," Mr. Logwood says. "I'll meet you there in a second."

They hang their heads, but before they walk away, they flash Toulouse and me spiteful looks. This isn't over.

"I'm sorry, Toulouse," Mr. Logwood says. "Please trust that the boys' behavior will not be tolerated."

Toulouse bows.

Mr. Logwood smiles, bows back, then walks away.

Toulouse reaches up and sets his gloved hand on my shoulder. *"Merci,"* he says, staring into my eyes for an uncomfortably long time.

"Sure," I say to break the trance.

It doesn't work.

By the time Mr. Logwood's talk with Garrett and Hubcap ends, the school day is over.

"We have to stay in for recess all next week because of you two little freaks," Garrett whispers menacingly when he returns.

Hubcap: "Yeah."

"You are *so* going to get it, Woody," Garrett says.

This is how they act after getting punished for being mean? Then again, what did I expect, sudden transformation?

The funny thing is that their threats don't bother me. Things have changed. Toulouse is my friend now, and somehow that makes me feel stronger, more comfortable in my oddness. It's harder to feel like a weirdo when there's someone who's as weird as you are. And it's harder for Garrett and Hubcap to scare me when I'm not facing them alone. And it isn't just Toulouse and me facing them. Lots of kids, including Monique and Ursula, stood up for us. And I bet Mr. Logwood will be doing more about the way they treat us than singing a little song.

But mostly things are different because I'm different. I feel braver. Stronger. I'm not going to let Garrett push me around, or put me down, anymore.

"When are we going to get it?" I ask Garrett. Again, I'm not stammering. "At recess?"

"No recess," Toulouse chirps.

Garrett's eyes flash with anger. Hubcap's, too.

I put my arm around Toulouse's very low shoulders. "Oh, that's right. You guys have to stay in during recess. All next week."

I grin.

28. Only Friend

"What are you making?" Willow asks me.

"You didn't knock," I answer.

"Sorry, what are you making?"

"You're supposed to knock before you come in."

"Do you want me to knock now?"

"It's a clutch."

"What's a clutch?"

"It's like a purse, only you hold it in your hand."

"No strap?"

"No strap."

"What's the point of a purse if it doesn't have a strap?"

"I don't know. It's not for me."

"Who's it for?"

"A girl at school. She asked me to make her one out of duck tape."

She pauses to think, then asks, "Will you make me one?"

"Sure."

"Do you still have the candy-corn duck tape?"

"Yup."

"I'd like mine made of that, please."

"After I finish this one."

"Who's the girl? Is she a friend of yours?"

"Her name is Monique."

"Isn't she the one you like?"

"She's okay."

"Was Toulouse at school today?"

"Yes."

"Was he nice to you?"

"Yes."

"Why don't you make him a clutch?"

"I don't think he'd want a clutch. He's a boy."

"Well, make him something he does want then."

I pause to think. If anyone deserves a

present from me, it's Toulouse. What would he like? Duck tape isn't really his style.

"You could make him a hat. He likes hats."

True, but his hats are so old-fashioned.

"I'll think of something," I say.

"Do the kids still make fun of him?" Willow asks.

"Not really. I think they're starting to appreciate him. They saw how good he is at painting, and at playing the accordion, and at hitting a volleyball."

"A volleyball?"

"Yeah. Garrett and Hubcap weren't impressed, of course. They kept on being mean to him. They called him names. They even got into his personal stuff."

"Oh!" she says, steamed. "Big bullies!"

Willow is very protective about her personal stuff.

"Exactly. Finally, Garrett knocked Toulouse's hat off, and I told him he was cruel and he needed to leave Toulouse alone. I had to protect Toulouse, you know?"

She nods seriously.

"Monique said Garrett was being mean, too."

"That's the girl you're making a clutch for?"

"Uh-huh."

"Does she like Toulouse?"

"I think she does. Then Mr. Logwood had a talk with Garrett and Hubcap, and they have to stay in for recess all next week."

"They deserve it!"

This makes me smile. I like how she stands up to injustice. I think she'll be better at it than I am.

"So everything's all right now?" she asks.

"Sure," I say, and laugh. Little kids can be so naive.

"And Toulouse is your best friend now?"

"He's really my only friend."

"No. I'm your friend, Woodman."

"Thanks, but that doesn't really count."

"Of course it *counts*."

She picks up a roll of duck tape with a pink zebra pattern.

"Can I make something, too?"

"What do you want to make?"

The last time I let her make something out of my duck tape, she ended up making a big wad of duck tape, then just walked away.

"I don't know," she says. "Maybe a purse? You know, with a handle? I could make the handle with the penguin duck tape."

"I don't have much left after your last project."

"See? We *are* friends. You're letting me have all your penguin duck tape."

"Maybe. Get a chair and I'll teach you how to make a purse, so you won't use up all of my pink zebra, too."

29. Wood

Toulouse lives in a tree house. A *tree* house. It's a house built into a *tree*.

His whole family lives in it, of course. The wood it's made out of still has the bark on it, which helps to camouflage the house—if that's what they were thinking when they built it. Most people's homes aren't camouflaged. I wish ours was. Theirs is so cool. I bet it's even harder to see when the trees aren't bare. In the spring, with the leaves, it must blend right into the wood.

The house isn't even on a paved road. They built it deep in the forest, away from everything, and everyone. There's no lawn or sidewalks or driveway. If they own cars, I don't see them. There are a couple of bicycles leaning against a neighboring tree. One of them has a covered trailer attached to it.

Toulouse meets me outside the house. He's wearing his suit and hat. He doesn't have his briefcase.

"Welcome," he says with a bow.

"Thanks," I say, and automatically bow back. I'm getting into the habit.

Following him, I climb the wooden spiral staircase that winds around the house's trunk, up to the front door. The knob is made of wood. Toulouse turns it and pushes open the door.

In the entryway, there's a wooden hat rack that looks like a tree. Its branches are the hooks, and the hooks are overflowing with hats. Toulouse starts to take off his hat, but then abruptly twists his head toward me, as if he forgot he had a guest. He ushers me into the next room, leaving the hat on his head.

I wonder why he changed his mind like that. Why doesn't he ever take it off? Is he hiding something under it? Is that why he hid under the desk when Garrett knocked his hat off?

We walk through a low archway into the

kitchen, which has a low, domed ceiling. His mom stands at the stove, wearing a long dress and old-fashioned lace-up boots. She's also wearing a pale pink bonnet with a ribbon that ties under her chin. It all seems a bit fancy for the kitchen.

She turns her head toward us without turning her body, like Toulouse does. She has large eyes, too, larger than Toulouse's, but then she's bigger than he is. She's not very tall, though. I think she's shorter than I am. She wears little granny glasses perched on her nose, which is as pointy as Toulouse's.

"Hello, Woodrow," she says, and curtsies. Her voice is deeper than Toulouse's, but just as flutey. Oboey, maybe. We studied the woodwind family last month in Mr. Weldon's class.

"Hello," I say. I don't want to call her Ms. Hulot in case I pronounce it wrong. Also, for some reason, "Ms." doesn't suit her. She seems too old-school for it. She's more like a "Mrs." Or, since she speaks French, maybe "Madame"?

She smiles and stares at me. I try to think of something to say. I laugh uncomfortably.

She looks at Toulouse.

"Come," he says, tapping my shoulder.

As we leave the kitchen, I look back at his mom. She's dropping something into the tall, steaming pot on the stove. It's small and gray with . . . fur?

Toulouse pulls me away and leads me up another spiral staircase, this one inside the house. On the next floor, which has ceilings so low I have to stoop over, we pass what must be his parents' bedroom. It's dark in the bedroom, and there appears to be someone in the bed, snoring. Toulouse presses a gloved finger to his pointy lips. He's telling me to be quiet.

"Papa works nights," Toulouse whispers.

"Mine, too," I say.

Toulouse's bedroom has a loft. He has to climb a ladder made of logs sawed in half lengthwise to reach his bed. No wonder he's so good at jumping: his house has a million steps. He has to literally climb into bed.

The next thing I notice about his room are his collections. He keeps things in old glass bottles and cases: bird nests, dead insects, pebbles, feathers of all sizes, bottle caps, rusty nails and screws, pull tabs, fish hooks . . . He also has a collection of small square bottles, empty but stained with ink, on his windowsill. He has several wooden fishing poles. They look hand-carved. There's an easel in the corner with a canvas on it. He's in the middle of painting a picture of the creek. It looks realer than the real thing.

I love his room. It reminds me of mine.

He picks up a rod and an old, sturdy tackle box. He gestures for me to follow.

We tiptoe by his snoozing dad, back down the spiral staircase. We stop in the kitchen.

"Salut!" he says to his mother, with a tip of his hat.

She says something in French in return.

He nods.

It must be fun to speak to your mom in another language.

30. Lunch

We walk through the wood toward the creek. It's Saturday morning, so we can take our time. We don't talk. We look at the trees and listen to the birds and our feet snapping the fir needles. The forest has a high ceiling, like the gym, or a theater. It's big and airy and still. It would be hard to climb these trees. The lowest branches are pointy stubs, way above our heads. The real branches are very high, reaching for sunlight.

At the creek, Toulouse and I sit side by side on a big log and open our tackle boxes. I show him some flies I made with duck tape.

"This one I made for you," I say. Making him a gift was Willow's idea, of course, but I don't mention that.

He takes it with a little bow and a *"Merci."*

"Why don't you try it out?" I ask.

He nods, then walks away to find his own waters.

I'm not wearing a watch. If Toulouse has his pocket watch, he doesn't check it, and I don't ask him to. Who cares what time it is? It's Saturday.

The sun keeps creeping across the sky, creating a slowly moving web of shadows over us and the creek. The morning goes by without bells or schedules, without standing in lines. It's Think Time all the time. Or maybe Not-Think Time. It's Silent Sustained Fishing.

My stomach tells me when it's lunch, not a clock or a bell or Mr. Logwood's schedule on the whiteboard. Toulouse and I return to the big log.

"Did you catch anything big enough to keep?" I ask. It's the first sentence I've said in a while, and it comes out gravelly.

I saw him catch quite a few fish. They all looked pretty small. I didn't notice him throwing any back.

He opens his wicker creel to show me it's empty.

"Toulouse?" I ask.

He looks up at me.

"Can I ask you a question?"

It's the Otto thing. I haven't been able to get it out of my mind.

"Did you . . . ? And then . . ."

I can't ask. I don't want him to think I'm accusing him of anything.

"Never mind," I say.

He nods, but keeps looking at me. Staring at me, really. It's like he wants me to ask him something.

I certainly have plenty of questions for him. There's a lot of things I don't understand. Like the furry golf ball he coughed up. And the way he appears and disappears so quickly. And the dropping out of trees without getting hurt. And the getting up them in the first place. And crossing the creek. There's also the way he turns his head around backward. And those weird diagonal lines in those huge, round eyes of his. Nobody's eyes are that big.

And his nose. Nobody's nose is that sharp. And, of course, there's the never taking off his hat, or gloves. I've never seen the top of his head, his hair, or his hands. Does he wear so many clothes because he likes to, or because he's hiding something?

And why didn't he want his picture taken? What was he afraid of? Is he a vampire or something?

He keeps staring me as I think about all of this, then at last he asks, "Food?"

He lifts the upper level of his tackle box and, from beneath it, takes out a sandwich wrapped neatly in wax paper.

I let go of my questions, and say, "Sure."

I brought along lunch, too: a PBJ and nacho-flavored tortilla chips. We unwrap our sandwiches and, at the same time, bring them up to our mouths. A tiny pink foot is dangling from his.

Toulouse senses me looking at the foot. He gives me the same look he did when he almost took off his hat.

And my mind starts putting things together,

coming up with answers to my many questions, answers that make sense but are completely, and insanely, impossible.

I set my sandwich on my lap.

"T-Toulouse?" I ask. "Are you . . . I mean . . ."

He tilts his head, listening.

"You're not an . . ."

I can't finish the sentence. It's too crazy. Of course he isn't. He can't be. He wears clothes. He goes to school. He reads. He paints. He plays the accordion. He can't be an . . .

But then again, it is all so *odd* . . .

"Woodrow?" he asks. "You okay?"

So *weird* . . .

"Woodrow?"

He inches over toward me. His legs don't reach the ground. He is so *little*.

Odd. Weird. Little.

O . . . W . . .

"Want some?" he asks, holding out his sandwich. The pink foot swings.

"I'm good," I say.

He's leaning in very close to me now. He blinks, and I see the diagonal lines again, one in each enormous eye. This is the closest I've ever gotten to him. His skin is fuzzy. No, not fuzzy. Not furry, either.

Feathery?

He smiles, nods, and tips his hat. All the way off his head.

And I see what he is.

31. Odd, Weird, and Little

I was right. What he is, is impossible. And crazy. And incredible. I suppose this is why I never saw it. Why no one did. Not even the adults: the teachers, the principal, not even Mom. If they did see it, they would have convinced themselves they didn't. It's too crazy. Too impossible. But if we had looked at Toulouse, really *looked* at him—past the weird grandpa suit and hat, the briefcase filled with so many odd things, his littleness and foreignness—we would have had to admit what he was.

And anyone who looked at him closely would feel what I'm feeling right now. Frightened. Shocked. Confused. As if suddenly all the rules we'd made up about the world were wrong. As if your own eyes couldn't be trusted. As if some weird dream you never had had came true. As if you had lost your mind.

I'm feeling and thinking all of these things at the same time. They are crashing down on me. I feel as if my brain is being wrung out like a rag, my heart is blowing up like a balloon, my legs have turned to rubber. Seeing how Toulouse is something that just can't be is changing me. I'm pretty sure I'm going to faint. Yep, here I go. . . .

"You okay?" Toulouse asks, bracing my arm with his gloved hand.

I jerk awake. I look at him. I really look at him.

And it's okay. I'm okay. More than okay. I feel proud. Proud that Toulouse showed me who he is. Proud that I was the first to see him. Proud to be his friend. I hope I am for a long time.

This will depend on who else discovers what he is. Imagine if Garrett found out!

No. No one must find out.

One thing's for sure. No one will ever find out from me.

"I'm okay," I say to Toulouse.

"Good," he says.

He dives into his sandwich. He doesn't chew. He swallows his food whole, pink foot and all.

Patrick Jennings

is the author of many popular novels for middle-schoolers, including *Guinea Dog, Lucky Cap, Invasion of the Dognappers, Guinea Dog 2*, and *Faith and the Electric Dogs. Guinea Dog* won the 2013 Kansas William Allen White Children's Book Award, the 2011 Washington State Scandiuzzi Children's Book Award, and received an honor in the 2013 Massachusetts Children's Book Award. That novel also appeared on the following state lists: the 2011 Colorado Children's Book Award, the 2010-2011 New Hampshire Great Stone Face Book Award, the 2012-2013 Florida Sunshine State Young Reader's Award, the 2014 Washington State Sasquatch Award, the 2014 Hawaii Nēnē Award, and the 2014-2015 Indiana Young Hoosier Book Award. He lives in a small seaport town in Washington State.

You can visit him online at www.patrickjennings.com.